Colours of Enlightenment

Right on Time

Sandeep Patel

Dedicated to live forever and have peace wherever.

Contents

Prologue

When a light ray is beamed into a right angled
triangular prism
the light is fractioned between 40° - 42° to reveal
seven distinct colours.
Newton (1672) first degreed this rainbow for five
colours;
red, yellow, green, blue and violet.
Only later he derived
orange and indigo
to match the colours to a musical scale:
C-D-E-F-G-A-B or C-B-A-G-F-E-D.

I: Family
BLACK

The night was still young. The snow had already fallen. The ground had cooled. To be asked to walk from the shades of streets darkened by dust or lack of light was imagined impossible as snow fell mostly all days of the year. The columns of buildings lined the streets of Moscow with blind out road markings that could not be seen even if they had happened to be painted in. Regardless with what had been studied; a large empire over the Himalayan Alps, covering much of Siberia, became Russia.

Nothing was occupied before the twenty-first century for most of Russia. Nothing could grow as the ground remained cold. Mostly cedars and pine trees covered in snow and patches of black mixed with the earth moving brought gray to several days. The land was bright but there was no light to shine through their environment into the naked pupil of a wondering eye. Indoors was the only place where the atmosphere could be greatly appreciated, not because these caverns were lit with log fires or that vodka was distilled to keep bellies warm, but because the animals prowling Russia warming in these caverns were men.

Practically everything that lived over the Himalayan Alps fell into coniferous trees in mixed forests giving a tundra terrain over the mountain one. Life members from the south vowed themselves to walk further north to find a new terrain and eastward they found a small stretch of water separating what we now know as North America from Asia. The terrain west was changed by the climate becoming colder. Finland was separated from Norway by Sweden, and each country established themselves from one another in the strong hold of the Russian Orthodoxy.

Regarding that the Russians existed to classify themselves for something that they believed in, they used their beliefs to breathe better. With practice and theory they calculated calm degrees of wind currents into measuring air flow to allow their blood to become saturated with oxygen easier. They learnt how to reside in the northern hemisphere together. Close to Finland, cities like Moscow and St. Petersburg, flourished as poppies with white petals. A delta flowed from the altitudes above Moscow and into the Black, and Caspian Sea. The stream of the water system dividing in two to reach a larger body of water was brought to life by Reko Moskva, which flowed through Moscow. Either side of the river lived the city.

Imagine close to a rhythm nothing but words in another language helping them get along and across oblivion. Music that rides along with bike tracks pressed into the snow intentionally hitting the awe. The feeling of music riding through his body from fogged shadows casting movement off walls of buildings over the metro as he rushed home. Beating over bumps that carry fog lights into eyes would hit him and us harder. The bright light would not reflect the road or a wall any better but carry on driving faster. Let go from the hand of grace, swift and the sudden left to save, not to tell where he had been, close your eyes and you shall see.

There he goes, and again, and again, gunshots fired for more than flesh, not crossed through a flake of quadriceps, but instead through the spleen with weight. Slowly now, and slowing down was not printed on his cards just as the ground he could not see. His road was static from the snow and shadow it's a mystery how he stayed free.

Practicing the will to become closer to Derrick Tarasov, worked to become worthy to speak of his will. The matter of fact was that he compelled to educate himself further; this was to understand how to get to know him better, to hear his conscious play music with the snow would make us fall in love with him forever.

Derrick was from some bay across the Isles, and across some pond, and into seeing Montreal from every glance around any corner he kept his mind on. There he shadowed himself from lights and ravens' caws as they shattered their shadows in synchronized form when casted metal bullets were fired from Moscow's haven.

New bullets can only be placed into new shells just as gunpowder can only be lit. Shine in between the horizon and between the air and edges of buildings. Crosses of cables along, along, along, and through each other as they fall back to where they came from. Refugees with music not sound, and with darkened creaking wood with insects that collect dust to hibernate in. Nicely lit with wax-and-wick, the candle kept alight as midnight oil burning to where the young man had to be going.

Flying over Tagansko-Krasnopresnenskaya Metro, from Sbarro, Derrick dropped his bike to his liking, and reacted with pupils dilating, along with a smile stretching to the sound of music beating from within his theatre. The clock had struck pass ten post meridiem in the first month of 2010. As he opened the door to his building the mix of cold and warm air sparked a shiver through his chest as he stepped inside.

II: Family

BLACK

Derrick's best friend, a megastar in his own right, and in his own name, a true talent to bring a cascade of fire down the forests of Russia. To be reckoned with volcanoes that spit ash to humidify areas close to trees without leaves like evergreens. Along with the earthquakes, the forest-fires allowed resolution, and from Kamchatka Peninsula, came evergreen lad Tyler Hussain. No matter how wide Tyler could see he always tried to look into gray, and what Tyler found was that in Russia hot springs brought cold floods.

Tyler prayed towards the walls of Moscow everyday. Standing beside Moscow Grand Mosque, he prayed by the wall and up close to master that the true horizon was only from above. He would attend prays to share what he had learnt from his beliefs to the younglings that only knew old language. A construction of a new mosque with light walls was to be established in celebration for a hundred year survival, Jumah Mosque. From where Tyler had seen the likelihood of expanding knowledge for the meaning of nothing could only be for the well.

Jumah Mosque would be more of a liking to Tyler once remodeling was done. Nevertheless standing for long hours in gray mists of cold was tolerated by most worshippers who prayed together and amongst each other. Waiting to exit Propekt Mira Metro, the time was to get the blood flowing back to his head. He rubbed his hands together even though they were in mittens and exhaled over his path. Propekt Mira was by the Moscow Grand Mosque, and prays were everyday from one till six. A pleasant probability of a fifty point average was hoped for Jumah Mosque to become refurbished with side seats and tables.

Hundreds of Muslims attended prays on times they felt comfortable attending. Most if not all days people would stand in the cold of Moscow avenues around the mosque to have pray. Mats stretched out onto the cold concrete stone foundation around Moscow Grand Mosque, and swift pray rituals throughout the day. If space was available indoors then people moved in without disturbing those who were already praying. A reconstruction to pull new generations to understand the needs to pray was the focus for a new mosque as Jumah.

Fasting Tyler could do without, nor alone did he only eat halal, not because of any religious verdict, or any verdict of religious letter, but as he didn't understand why that he should eat. Closing in from his diet Tyler gave thanks and ate well. He aided in assistance with Derrick on relaying on his judgment as close to any friend can have on one. What Tyler harnessed was the darkness in a flame and that flame was ignited through Derrick. As with any being the existence can only be by the existence of another, and as for one being the only other was communism. Meaning diplomatist around Moscow would be in better understanding to thank another communist. It would just be easier if everyone could trust one another. Just like these friends', their souls would never spend time without one another.

Tyler's fuel was poured from his knowledge and harnessed by his love to read. Also he joined rampaging crowds of supporters watching the Soviet Union change from athletes for war to patient grazers of ice for the Russian Hockey Federation. From the wooden box and screen within Derrick's basement theatre, Tyler would watch the National Hockey League of the United States, and admire how the best there, were not at all as close to the best of all Russian twig and biscuit leagues.

So from escalating cheers and chants of victories to calming whispers and echoes in the wind, Tyler Hussain, maintained in spirit as Muhammad Ali, maintained righteous worship in transition to be delighted in being called Cassius

Marcellus Clay, once again. Forever passing through eternity and through the metro rails of Moscow, Tyler studied within dimly lit libraries, strobe movie cuts and illuminated walls of religion. Praise was only to one, and to that one Tyler shared time with when he wished to relax and pay thanks to where he knew passion rested.

III: Family
BLACK

Turgenevskaya Metro was attached to Chistye Prudy Metro, where the orange line met the red one. That stop was the one used to unwind Tamana from thoughts of work, and was used to born the reasons for one to live life, i.e. to reapply dried lip gloss. That one stop was also used to remove the day's mutiny, reflect immediate rescue to be taken by wisdom, and to neglect the day's events to affecting her relationships to who she was to have coffee with. From Medvedkovo, Tamana would travel to meet Derrick arriving from Cherkizovskaya, to meet her at Chistye Prudy, before meeting Tyler inside Okhotny Ryad Metro.

Dark hair mostly jet-black with a few blonde streaks waved with a lift that most models would crave to have had Tamana. Smooth northern skin with a hint of Portuguese tan left by inheritance from her grandfather covered her all over. Full bodied lips, long eyelashes and a perfectly occluding white sparkling dentition, an athletic body accompanied with dark hazel eyes in a sea of corneas, and to match all a thirst for knowledge alongside a fast right hook.

17

Looking like a million dollars scratch free and unmarked was never to be affected even with a poor diet for Tamana. Overall most days of the year Tamana was covered by different fabric scarves, wooly hats, mittens or leather gloves, large black coats and boots to match. The only personality seen on the surface from a stranger would be a stern appearance on thoughts she would have had been having throughout her day. These thoughts would be a mixture of her work or her past.

So the three of them would meet in amongst hundred others to exit the station. Okhotny Ryad Metro led out to Lomonsov Moscow State University, where the three of them studied. Around Red Square, and the Kremlin, sat millions of years of knowledge, never minding that the university held the second largest number of books in Russia. An amazing amount of life kept the university holding sixty-six thousand bodies of power alive.

Tamana was born Russian Orthodox, being aware of the history their city had struggled from forest-fires to warlords. Blessed was she to be born into a strong household in Moscow. Tamana Rostova, loved to visit the old monuments celebrating St. Basil the Blessed prophecy. She admired things that she fully could not understand; this she felt brought meaning into her life.

18

From reading the start of the magnificent Cathedral Square, to accommodate beauty and afterlife, that the Ninth Chapel was built to grave St. Basil, beside St. Basil's Cathedral. Before the Ninth Chapel was built St. Basil rested on the site of Pokrovsky Cathedral, a.k.a. St. Basil's Cathedral; nine chapels were founded on Trinity Cathedral over Okhotny Ryad.

Moscow Kremlin was beside the Red Square, and homed two cathedrals and a chapel to tighten trinity hope in Moscow from forest-fires, wars and earthquakes. Alongside Reko Moskva important and incredible drops of heaven stand watching the water flow through the city. The mentality of fifteen century humans built more. One that Tamana joined with her family was through the Metropolitan Peter, which was built initially during 1475-1479, but was torn down once built and when refurbished an earthquake tore it down once more. The building was built once more and now is known as Dormition Cathedral at Moscow Kremlin.

At times Tamana would travel with Derrick to Aleksandrovsky Sad Metro, have lunch and walk over Red Square back to Okhotny Ryad, or to work at the European Medical Center at Tverskaya Metro. She would begin to ask Derrick weird questions to find reasons on what kept the buildings intact. He would not know much about the reason for why they were built, but relied on love that kept them standing. Head over heels Tamana was over Derrick. Her thoughts ran for her to return to sleep close to the hospital and luckily close to him by Tverskaya Metro.

Tamana had two frequent occurrences in her life, both that she enjoyed. One was sweet kisses shared between the hospital and her beeper, and the other was sweet kisses shared with her boyfriend. She had found her foundation relationship with a healthy social life and a hectic working life, which was made easier by Derrick allowing her to have a key to his place. He was the only person that she was close to as a friend and as a person. Everyone else surrounding her life like her hospital family was loved, but anytime she had away from rotations she spent catching up on sleep.

When her thoughts became her own she wondered about her brother. Her one and only brother left the family when she was close to fifteen and spent time working abroad with the Russian Army. There had been no contact after the fall out between her father and him that there were no letters sent in either direction, frankly Tamana had no idea if her brother was still alive or not. Hence she studied into a full working career to keep her mind occupied, and she hugged Derrick tighter when she began to expect the worst for the one she loved the most.

Krasnaya Ploschad, a.k.a. Red Square. 'Krasnaya' meaning, 'beautiful', was paved in the seventeenth century on the high altitudes of where Moscow resides. A beautiful red image throughout the sky reflected light of the sunrays to hit the clouds that reflected a strong red light over the ground of Moscow, giving the ground its name.

Tamana, Derrick and Tyler knew everything there was to know about each other. Their love for one another was strong and lived to ease concern from outside interferences. In laymen's term they looked out for each other. If the three were not together then they would be at prays, working, exercising or spending time on the interests that they had. Tyler would attend prays and at all other times with Derrick. Tamana would either be with Derrick, or with faculty members of the university and sick people. Derrick would mostly be at the university's archives or humming to himself behind the screens of the New Opera Theatre, jotting new ideas of interests with his surplus supply of black ballpoint pens on blank paper, or white chalk on several non-rotating sixty-inch blackboards. The dust settles as the dawn rises till the day falls back to dusk where the friends work for no more dust as the dawn rises.

IV: Life
VIOLET

Venezia Restaurant, served the best Italian food for any person especially those close to veterans. The restaurant sat close to the theatre and if Derrick Tarasov was not ordering pizza in then he would order creamy bacon and mushroom fettuccine pasta from Strosney Boulevard's Venezia's. One phone call with half an hour waits for warm food or a ten minute dash, voluntary conversations, tasters in mind and food sealed to stay hot for his ten minute dash back to his villa in the basement of the theatre.

Working with values of each other and violet lily storks resting on Derrick's table, through watching the monitor of his television glow violet light to lighten his living quarters, he was not to be seen as he was closely camouflaged into his surroundings. Derrick's thinking gowns were not uniforms like lab coats or hard helmets with a tool belt, but was one shirt. The only shirt the he wore when he sat alone at home, a light shade between purple and pink collars he wore with buttons of the same shade to match, and thread dyed on the same shade. He felt well spending time by amusing himself with comedy when trying to keep his brain waves working. So he wore his shirt hiding himself from the light of the television and the flowers on his table, and thought of the values he had for Tyler Hussain and Tamana Rostova.

In early years the friends of three grew around graffiti painted on mostly every surface of their surroundings. The suburban housing estates would often receive a handful of paint. Some were valued respectably whereas others were tags by local gangs that feared vengeance from the local law enforcement; however both groups of artists forced themselves not to rush their work. Any implementation of reapplying great or better art was offered condolences by the communities to have their art kept for longer. The artist would learn, adapt, practice, and strengthen their works of art just as flowers, like numerous violas species breeding to survive.

From a very long time ago, from a time when young lads were lost to value love, from a time when men thought reading was not cool, from exchanging approval of varied values of trust Derrick and Tyler had got to know the other. From the age of twelve they had shook hands and shook aerosol cans. They repainted surfaces white to improve their skill when all was blackened out. Luminous violet was their shade as this was ambiguous to the nightlight. Their tags were totally represented for recognition as they tagged three hundred foot train carriages. No matter what time Derrick would call on Tyler to keep guard he did as the other painted onto the carriages. When two limbs tired or when two lungs filled with enough toxins to make one of the brothers faint they would shift rotations to ensure their mark was finished. The last project of painting dark galloping horses with light manes in black and violet proved to be their most memorable.

As for the third musketeer; Tamana knew very well of the boys since she was young and found encouragement to listen in with Derrick's mother in the kitchen. Her life had been as beautiful as Christina Aguilera, her valentine Derrick Torosov to always be forever. Medvedkovo was where she was from; Krasnosel'skaya was where he was from; however vibrations from Derrick's and Tamana's views with Tyler had gained reputation amongst their peers from Shchelkovskaya to Yugo-Zapadnaya.

A delivery was received one night when Derrick had to catch up to his artwork and sign his sentence before the carriages began moving. Unfinished work, but the carriages were back the next night unexpectedly as the adolescents were painting other surfaces like vents, meter boxes and the valet sections of virgin trains. The previous night's work had been left outside the train garage inviting a perfect opportunity for Derrick and Tyler to pursue the thought of reason. Was the train left outside because it's soon to be in service? Was the train left out the garage because it needed to be cleaned? Was the reason that due to humid summers the controller felt shy not to park it inside? Or was the train delivered from God to help them express their work to a wider Moscow? As the previous night's work had departed into the tunnels of Moscow metro as unfinished, the pink-purple violet paint from the aerosols had to be packed in haste regardless of the paint drying; the lads had jumped the fence just in time to see the rear lights of the train disappear into the darkness. The paint on the returned carriages had dried and was retouched with their two colours just as they had started; the art was finished with ideal calligraphy along the same side of the remaining train carriages. The horses were stern to the finish leaving room for their signatures.

V: Life
VIOLET

Through where Derrick kept his vase of flowers there laid paper work across most of the floor in his new home from Krasnosel'skaya to Tverskaya. Along with his own plants of exotic colours Tamana had brought him her own. The violet lilies brought life to Derrick's inspiration, along with a fold out couch-bed, and enough space to allow room for more paper work to fall in. Living for his idea he was not shy of cash but shy to embarrass his Father. Through his own experience he placed his Father's words to practice and marvelous things began to happen.

The other plant in the room was a clematis flower. The flower had its own vase and the flower was replaced unknowingly. As the three of them circled away and into the New Opera Theatre, rotationally reaching to adulthood the flowers always seemed to bloom. There was plenty of space for Tyler to live with Derrick, as for no apparent reason besides the escape of reality for Tyler's past and Derrick's love for him. Tamana loved Tyler as Brendan Fraser would love to keep valuing that flowers remained vertical.

Usually Tyler would sit on a beanbag and entertain himself with videogames and books. Now the men were old enough to appreciate that silent company was golden, and with this respect Tamana was considered mostly like them. Within Derrick's living quarters some areas were decorated venerably, Tyler had added a few photos of women torn out of magazines to decorate Derrick's coffee table with. Tamana also placed photos of herself amongst the growing wall of glossy pages. Derrick had no pictures of people, just pages of black ink sometimes as words, sometimes as diagrams or sometimes as equations.

The kisses between Tamana and Derrick began once Tamana had received an official position at the medical centre. She was just as the men realized, she was as cool as she would be versatile. And by far there is no doubt about a little bit of hugging, a little bit of kissing and a little bit of loving. If this needs to be speculated then the hugging came from Tyler, the kissing came from Derrick and the loving came from above, as most likely Tamana would have been a vigilante.

Living close to sun beds was not desirable for most people in Russia, however there were few who would rather bathe directly in sunlight. Going far enough to feel relaxation that one person could sleep without being disturbed in broad daylight came as a surprise. This fault would lead to possibly laying around for longer and through a ray of light as ultraviolet burn a hole close to the infraorbital nerves of the trigeminal maxillary branch, cranial nerve V. The burn from a ray of light not the heat, the fixed position of laziness, unlike distinguishing shorter wavelengths than that of the hue of Derrick's shirt, can lead to malignancies. A necrotic development of automatically degrading cells later following the nerve to indefinitely erode the outer ear, but most soon likely the loss of vision, personally whined the violin. The metro station to the emergency room in Moscow is pronounced as Tagansko-Krasnopresnenskaya. The gift shop takes VISA for flowers as clematis, tulips and orchids.

"Would they be able to see me if they were around? And what if I sat absolutely still?" he thought to himself. "Where would we go from here?" Derrick mindfully asked whilst mapping himself an answer.

Mapping was performed by first having the hands together at fingertips, or staring at an open palm protected by other palm, and then pushing the vision into the horizons of perplexes. Derrick moved his fingers through each other and out from one another with this view, sometimes with hands close to touch, and sometimes away from his body like he was describing why his victim should stand on guard.

Over and over again Derrick read words through the digits and palms of his hands. Multitude of times variables changing, expanding, stretching, climbing, falling like charting vectors on maps. All concluding to non-variable factors, like when and how the final line of mapping would be drawn, as a conclude thumbs up, as a strike through his words, as a stop from dance of his fingertips to attract his indexes, or a value to closing on a word scribed by his thumb on his pinky. He flicked his right pinky on his left and drifted away to another view.

VI: Intimacy
BLACK

Good things don't usually fall out of thin air nor do they fall from somewhere far. These matters of principle become evident when they were to be matched. The sounds of popping firecrackers, beating drums, chattering people, and the unzipping of Tamana's dress was heard as they amused love far from Moscow in the year 2011.

She held herself tight to allow no resistance for Derrick to unveil her beauty easily. The beat of their hearts pounded in one rhythm as they undressed each other. Kissing and holding themselves close to one another in case the other at that very moment would try to escape. They brushed fingertips along the other's body. Pulling back the top four buttons Tamana forced back Derrick's shirt and slowly unbuttoned the rest just to touch a damp vest. He helped her with the sleeves and slipped off her dress to the floor.

Both concealed in the bodies of Adam and Eve they began to experiment with each other. A warm wind blew the curtain drapes a float and caused the impulse of their action to fall into more comfortable pressures.

Derrick laid over Tamana and kissed her curves from breast through to pelvis. She placed her toes on his chest and kicked him back to stand; unbuckling his buckle she climbed her weight onto his shoulders kicking his pants to the floor with her tongue in his mouth. Derrick grabbed hold of her below the waist line with one arm and climbed out of his foot holes.

He found it amusing letting her bra fall free. She touched herself to warm Derrick further. He pushed her onto the wall beside the air vent and stood erect as the sweat from their bodies raised goose-bumps on excitement.

The evaporated air chilled their skin further making them hold each other tighter. She tried to turn herself away from him but he marked her move to plant her above him. They covered the night in pleasuring each other all through to the morning where the firecrackers were still crackling.

Their souls had intertwined both mentally and physically. They lived with each other knowing very well of their lives. The believed in living for the a God, for a Light, this light was their life that they were presented to live. Both of them required peace, Tamana through her work and Derrick through the thought of his future. This peace was felt to be entertaining when they realized blinking at each other, eye contact was considered cool and cool was considered anything coloured black. Black was peaceful to their eyes. Love was red for them and red was identified as the colour for blood. Red was everyone and every creature on the planet. Derrick and Tamana entertained themselves believing that their lives were not theirs for the keeping. The monopoly of love was conquered as they closed their eyes from the light coming from outside.

The rest of their time together was to be equally spent in one another's kama. To hold each other in body, mind and spirit before reaching karma for eternal life. For her not to be valued close to prophetess widowed he hoped that death would approach her before that arriving on him. Well established was Derrick's love that was shared with Tamana's. However within the darkness of their surrounding they both knew that this love was not theirs to keep. The morning sunlight passed from seven till eleven ante meridiem missing the window frame which darkened the floor as a shadow of their keeper.

VII: Leisure
INDIGO

T hings were impossibly imagined when they came between an indigo cushion and a purple cloth. Instead of denying the lines under a completely different shade of hue as those running metros in other cities, there was no denying the importance implied by this colour. Also seen when iodine solutions are added to starch residues.

As the sky changes colour for no grounds to be played, when everyone's asleep, slowly whisper in my ear, trick or treat. Play slow whispers covered in your own time with us, and we shall pray together when called upon. Tip-toe into sweet quarters, and around tip-toe for awhile between plays, and pray with others as they watch the curtain close. One time, last rhyme, to keep the earth turning for all time. Most likely the earth would stop turning and everything including the trees would be pulled inwards. Brace yourself listening as you begin to listen to softer echoes whilst we pray together.

Pull out a large glass, one with a large rim enough for a golf ball to fall in. Replace with ice cubes. Pour concentrated blackberry syrup to inch over the ice cubes. Pour the water, pour the water, shake with stirrer. Drink slowly. Possibly, possibly remove ice cubes and drink by the gallon, three cups per ten seconds should keep them blooming like berries. Furthermore an act of action potential can be ignited as that existing between samurai warriors, like Uma Thurman and Lucy Liu, a current that can result indirectly to melt an igloo.

There was a place once where the colour reflecting from the light shining off the walls was a chapter. The chapter was a part of an active lifestyle covered by tools needed to mould strength into the mind. A cool desire for curiosity why learning was actually cool. Chromosomes splitting indefinitely resulted to men forgetting that it was learning that moved them. Usually the only sentence that needed no explanation was, 'if it's not the wall then it's black,' but that place has made this chapter the wall and the rest of the story our time. More pound of meat on cattle as they graze royally to be served.

Hmm, mmm, aaa, ooo, investigate, eradicate, just scratch over once, carry into the next interstate. A purple fish is a Purple Fish swimming in the seas around the Caribbean singing a song. Like an Indigo Hamlet found in the Caribbean, a carnivores fish eating shrimp and feeder fish, or like a bird as an Indigo Bunting being more of deep blue with striped black wings. La, la, la, you know lady holding those deep marine tulips. Love Lauryn Hill as Wyclif Jean, and Anderson Police keeps us on the ground for fair lady as delicious as a bar of Cadbury.

VIII: Leisure
INDIGO

Who likes short shorts? They like short shorts! Who likes short shorts? They like short shorts! Who likes short shorts? Nevertheless these shorts were not possible to wear at all in Moscow. Most likely they could be bought from a mall and worn around the home, but as cold as everything was behind closed doors there was no reason to wear those shorts at all, (even though they were liked in every colour especially that of purple). The short shorts were left to their imagination and let whomever wearing the short shorts keep them on, or protected over with chance that the short shorts do not become too short. We like short shorts!

Tyler would sometimes meet Derrick waiting for his food at the restaurant opposite the theatre. A side of Greek Kalamate Olives was ordered with his pasta.

"What's up with the olives man?" he asked.

"A – men!" replied Derrick.

Tyler paused for a second and reached over to grab himself a toothpick to pierce the side of an olive; he looked at it and took a bite. Derrick looked at him whilst he enjoyed the olive. Tyler looked at the end of the other half of the olive and raised his eyebrows. Staring at his piece of nectar he pierced and ate another one. Sucking in the juices that enriched his mouth he placed the left piece of olive and allowed to let sit on his tongue, savoring the flavor he took a few bites into the olive's dark flesh and swallowed.

"Nice, really, not so much my style, but possibly. How's work coming along? Anything else He needs you have me know, and spring me another twenty-thousand for smooth coverage," Tyler said.

"That's no problem; retirement fund is a sure thing to spend."

Derrick looked over the table to where they were and moved the pepper jar. A waitress came walking to place his take out on the table.

"Can I have another portion of those olives?" ordered Derrick.

"I will place them to go as well," she said.

"Next thing I know you will be buying grapes," Tyler laughed.

"A – ma'am!" the waitress replied at Tyler, and walked away.

Neither of them usually ate fruits. Their diets were small amounts of oil, with complex carbohydrates as pasta and potatoes, plus fats and protein within meat, furthermore milkshakes with loads of calories. The sound mind brothers were large and filled out, exercised well and drank plenty of water. Their diet just as their minds were not considered something important to argue over. They ate well and they shared most things over the other, and interestingly enough they both began to like kalamate olives. They were never shy of cash, so flesh from an animal came for the same price as flesh from a fruit; hence there was no mental confusion between eating cuts of meat or baskets of plums.

"Whose bra is that on the cross? Whose bra is that on the cross? Is that your bra on the cross? Is that your bra on the cross? Jesus, whose bra is that on the cross? Jesus, whose bra is that on the cross? That's Mary's bra on the cross. That's Mary's bra on the cross. Why's your bra on the cross? Why's your bra on the cross? 'Cause all that's mine is on the cross. 'Cause all that's mine is on the cross!" chanted Derrick to amuse Tyler on their walk back.

"I don't know what you've been told, there's one God, and no devil," carried on Tyler and whistled the military melody.

To keep everything and mostly anything alive was to prove its existence. Two serpents wrapped around a sword was most definitely a path to deliverance but what if the music stopped? As for Tamana, she would demonstrate this through pulling out all sorts of stuff from unconscious throats when they arrived to her emergency room from drowning, or choking, or a shortness of breath, or any other reason for being purple. Yes, they like short shorts and they like them indoors, they incredibly never like ignorance so they help anyone swim deep rather than fall.

IX: Friends
BLACK

The ambulance was tainted with snow that fell every night across the winter. The snow left the lights to blink black and white as the vehicle moved through the streets of Moscow. Craig was standing opposite the New Opera Theatre warming up. He had to catch the train from Pushkinskaya Metro, to home across the northwest to Begovaya.

Craig Goncharov, was in his early thirties. He was dressed in a large, dull, dirty, beige coat. The reason for why the coat was dirty was because he lived in the slumps of Moscow without any soap. The reason for why the coat was dull was because he had slept in the beige pigment of polyester the coat was woven from. And the reason for why the coat was large was because he never negotiated with the life that he had been presented with. His head was covered by a wooly hat and bags of facial hair representing a beard or a hiding spot for any weapons of mass destruction. He stood at 5'11" wearing gloves with worn out finger holes and boots that were close to barking. With natural denim heavy cargo jeans and a moth breathing woolly jumper overlying any all day and everyday use undergarments he stared into the darkness, he stared into the darkness and rested to wait for the light.

The shutters of private stores were being shut. Pitched screens of street light identified the serpent and sword image on the side of the emergency vehicle. Snow kept falling and Craig noticed Derrick entering the theatre with heavy boxes. Abram, the doorman was helping Derrick hurry in a ton of weight. Silently the ambulance crossed his sight with lights' flashing.

A torso framing close to an equilateral triangle with larger limbs than normal, Abram Shiraz, stood at 6'3" covering a circumference of a baby elephant. He wore a light gray jacket with collars stiffened as when French soccer star, Eric Cantona, had when playing for Manchester United. His shoe size, his weight, and his gait prevented him from easily slipping on the iced ground, however if he had a shake and fell, he would be felt for several yards and possibly a crane would be needed to lift him back to his feet. For a well dressed, well spoken, extremely healthy individual there were only a few he could look up to and believe on. One was his faith in Derrick, and the other was with his faith in Christ, Son of God.

He believed in Derrick Tarasov, as Derrick only preached what he read and learnt. From all the people that Abram Shiraz spoke with, Derrick was likely to speak with accuracy and with noble truth. Derrick also believed Jesus was staked high so that they would have someone to look up to. So they looked up to see Jesus on telephone poles as strobes of flashes as the snow carried on falling.

Before he was blessed in meeting Derrick, Abraham's father had encouraged him to worship well for others. Through the stories listed in the New Testament, the devotion the Apostles had for Jesus was one to be admired by Abram. Unlike a million others Abram's born belief was followed by thought and action to his devotion.

Around any major city the homeless would live and Moscow too had its fair share. They would find sleep in tight corners of walls and warm pockets of air under bridges of Survorosky Park, and up north to Park Vorob'evy Gory, all the way through to Nats Park. Into Moscow city sat these parks surrounding the Cathedral Square and the Kremlin. The river flowed like soft metallic silver across the night through Moscow and under the ambulance at times. The gray scale of St. Basil's Cathedral was reflected by the river with the distinguishing patterns moving with the water, but no colours could be seen. Unlike roads built from the day of the Romans', the roads of Moscow city were always tried to be kept clear.

Inside the emergency vehicle, the paramedic held on tight and tried to stop darkened blood pouring onto the floor of the ambulance. The pool of blood gathering on the floor was tried not to be slipped on. The paramedic cut open a patient's jeans. She held onto a silver handle as she felt a sudden stop to come shortly.

A person had fallen off the wall of a fountain trying to collect the rubles that others had thrown in. He grinded his thigh skidding down into the water and almost pierced his superficial femoral vein as he shifted past a fountain spoke. One ruble was approximately three cent, where the person had many five ruble coins, and regardless none were to be replaced back into the fountain. He wondered why the people threw their money away like that. The person began to wish the thought of throwing some rubles back into the fountain as soon as he got well.

Shifting weight the paramedic held the patient down and covered his leg with a cloth. She administered him with morphine intravenously into one of the antecubital veins for an immediate response. The patient felt alleviated from pain and began to breathe slightly softer. She placed a mask over his mouth and nostrils and fed him hundred-percent oxygen. Mostly children with asthma were gently administered oxygen when they would be having an anxiety attack. She exhaled forcefully down and away from the patient for a few seconds instead to catch fresh oxygen in her breath.

Nevertheless the patient rushing through the streets of Moscow would be well. The morphine saturated into his blood had placed him into a strobe within the ambulance that allowed the patient to forget his situation. The paramedic driving yelled for them to brace.

Moving away from Craig Goncharov the ambulance did not have far to go. The hospital fell round the corner from where the snow carried to fall and obscure Derrick's notice on Craig.

"Come inside and have something to eat before you leave Abram. Have got some steak in the freezer I'll stick on the pan," asked Derrick.

"Another time Dee, it's about four in the morning. I'm waking on the crack of dawn tomorrow, then seeing you in the evening."

Derrick grabbed the last box away from the side entrance to the theatre from Abram and moved it inside. He came back outside and looked up at the falling snow. Abram had already sat in the van and had started the engine. Derrick looked around the street and inhaled, he closed the doors to the side-entrance with a loud thud. Craig watched with amazement until the doors closed. He wondered what was fueling the men to struggle with heavy cargo in the middle of the night that he decided to break into the building the following night.

X: Friends
BLACK

"Good afternoon, Derrick," said Abram. "Good afternoon, Abs. Let you know this straight away; surely the real under the thumb is not as great as the knife I can pierce Him with. Come downstairs and help me arrange a few things and make sure the doors are locked at night. The doors are locked because I too want the spider outside feeding, nesting, eating, living without audio, outside." Derrick said.

"Hmmm …"

"To keep them wondering, but that is what I attend to change. Found the key to paving His time to the next best point. Easily help me down these stairs, and easily curve through the sun's gravity to the area where I choose. Now we can go round, but not north or south in space, around to where the earth would have sat where I choose. You can take a choice too. Go on take a pick in time."

"What do you mean man?" replied Abram.

"Anytime you wish from minus infinity to plus infinity. There is no point catching your own death if that is what you were thinking? I have tried this once and you would I have said?"

"Well when is it?"

"That's right. And not going to let you know just yet, you believe me you have nothing to look forward to," finished Derrick on Abram's zen.

They headed to switch on the theatre lights and moved upstairs to the chairman's office. Abram placed a few things as his gloves, keys and hat on the table. Careful not to scratch the mahogany wood he moved the items clockwise, (this was for no reason except to spend a second of time), and then he turned around himself to hear Derrick begin talking.

To what Derrick was to Abram was his bread and butter. This man had something of an admiration placed upon him, and was not shy to deliver that admiration for his people. Abram was a large man with darker skin than most Russian natives, and brought wisdom to the people that he surrounded. Derrick admired Abram as Abram prayed whenever he found time. Derrick intentionally began praying anywhere facing south as he believed the Lord looked up at earth from heaven. Abram believed as him and at times would bow south to pray and then switch north to see what the Father was watching. Overall the light of heaven lights a dark room as a candle lit in its center, the whole room is illuminated, but still the two friends wished for their Father to look up at them as children would do for adults.

46

Grab the nail with the left hand, and spin upwards with a strong grip hold of other hand on the hammer, on the recovery strike through. His Father was the Father of Jesus, which made Him Abraham's Father. Baffled about this, so he decided to place the blood of Jesus to the test. However there was no need to have him dragging the stake up the mountain or was that Him imitating Derrick? Three nails please and let's mount Him up! Climb the mountain by tensing the left pectoral major and left scapula region, the cross just lifts itself. They helped him climb a few steps and then He was there. And now Derrick was thinking what he should do next. After finding the truth about Tyler and Tamana, the only possibility would be to live ten yards ahead of everyone else.

"Once you're done here, and everyone is out, and you have locked up thoroughly, after every last member of staff have left safely home, you let her know that she will have to meet you later at the Sheraton. Here's the key for tonight only. Tomorrow you are going to choose from all the colours that Moscow has to offer. And these game tickets," Derrick looked over at Abram.

"Okay," he said.

"Take your time, no rush, not going anywhere anytime soon. Wait till the friends are there and flirt with the woman in the deep indigo dress, there'll be one in a gray dress, and another in a blue one. They all have the eyes for you tonight, so just slap your own thigh when you need some alone time. You work this how you want."

Derrick handed Abram the keys and Abram pointed to push his heart.

"But first downstairs with the fool, and nothing on your mind except sleeping with the naked broad tonight. You understand right?" asked Derrick.

"I don't know what you are talking about, but I'll be there tomorrow," replied Abram.

Derrick closed the job description for that evening's lineup and handed them to Abram. Collecting his thoughts by staring to the ground Derrick finalized the work for the week's plays at the theatre. Abram placed his belonging to hand and left Derrick's side to open the theatre for that night's performance. Derrick came out of thought after Abram had left and gathered his notes to the basement. A multi-networking array of work and play kept the friends occupied throughout all times of the day. That to rest the mind at anytime was foolish unless they wished to start back at the beginning.

XI: Friends
BLACK

Within the basement of the New Opera Theatre, Tamana, Tyler and Abram arrived to see Derrick. Derrick's living space was clean for the first time the friends had known him there. They had noticed that the piles of paper and scraps of notes that usually decorated the place were all missing, they did not think to ask Derrick why his place was tidy, but they did appreciate that they did not have to mind their step around his home.

"Alright guys don't become too surprised; you are going to see someone more amazing than me. Tyler, Tamana, Abram brace yourselves. Seriously you guys need to sit down. Don't become too used to liking me, but gather that I like you, and I like them, so let me rejoice you with some others," said Derrick.

"What are you talking about?" she said.

Abram had moved already to the couch and had sat down. Tyler noticed Abram sitting and walked over to sit with him. Derrick smiled slightly and moved Tamana to sit with them and moved back. He looked at all three of them and they remained gazed at him.

"Okay guys you can come to see yourselves," said Derrick to thin air.

From the other end of Derrick's home, over a corner step that opened the kitchen, in which the pantry was, walked out Tyler and Abram stepped in light from behind the door, and Tamana from within the closet came to slowly stand facing themselves sitting on the couch. The friends sitting on the couch sat with their mouth's wide open starring at the new comers.

"Don't faint," said Tamana to herself.

Tyler stood up to look closer at himself.

Abram sat on Derrick's seat staring at Derrick. He looked slightly at himself.

"Indigo," Abram said to himself sitting on the couch.

Abram on the couch looked over at Derrick. The three new comers waited fingers and thumbs. From the kitchen came another shadow. They all looked over to see another Derrick eating a bowl of cereal.

"I'm the real one, meaning your time, our time, and he's my future part, have you told them the news?" asked Derrick to himself. "I can let some stranger wake me in my sleep but to then offer him my food?"

"Ha ha ha ha. Ha ha ha!" they both laughed.

"Yes I hope they understand. Please take a moment to write down the appearance of our departure. Need to record the area of subatomic aura around us as we leave into thin air, 'well out of waves of magnetism that hold the world turning with the sun.' That is an extremely small number, but regardless I have maintained a force to move the flow of electromagnetic waves all the way from earth to the sun safely. Let alone the release has allowed me to travel through time. Wish I could travel through space," Derrick began laughing to himself, and the other Derrick began to chuckle with him.

The friends of present and future sat observing themselves closer. Incredible to comprehend the actions of oneself to be seen in direct contact, that all the friends sat in silence momentarily without tempering with the other. They smiled voluntarily to provoke a response from themselves as time passed, and to notice that the Derrick's were consumed in their own conversation to care nonetheless for their surprise.

"We were trying to find more effective ways to raise empty pallets," added future Derrick. "Lifting pallets was always tricky than heavy, and I thought what about a manual lift by using forces to pulse pallets off the ground so we can move them easier."

"But instead of moving pallets, I found that decreasing the weight of the object to be moved decreased dramatically around the machine, which I worked to become a time-machine," continued present Derrick. "I'll take the notes as you leave Dee."

"You just wanted to say your own name there didn't you? Go, Derrick!" said future Derrick.

They all smiled at each other and looked at the future Derrick. He moved over to the three future friends and they braced his shoulders as they had traveled before. He unhooked a metal staff from his possession and pressed the surface with his left forefinger. A few seconds past and the room began to get colder. A chill was evident to them as frost would have been to a rattlesnake. They all held each other tightly, whilst he held the staff tightly, Abram held him tighter and they vanished to leave naked air leaving the other four.

XII: Friends
BLACK

Later on that same night once everything had been performed and tested, after witnessing themselves come and go, Tyler thought to pray with his family, Abram knew to take Derrick's word and head to Sheraton Hotel, and Tamana grabbed hold of Derrick as they all left ahead of Abram locking the doors of the theatre. The time was early on the next morning after Craig had seen Derrick last. Abram double checked the lock and moved in over to Derrick's other shoulder.

"That was a real good show," said Abram, "Thanks man."

Tamana kissed Derrick and he rocked slightly left and right. Tyler opened his left hand and looked at the sky reflecting off his palm; he scrolled the light off his fingers and looked over at Derrick to point to his heart. The feeling they must have all experienced was uncountable. They embraced each other and walked down the street in anticipation for warm freshly baked pizza.

"Mmm, smell it now, mama's got something cooking in the oven," rhymed Tamana.

"I'll make sure to save you a slice when I see you Ab in the morning," said Derrick.

"Now that makes two of you or shall I say one? No, no, there were three now saying the same. Listen Dee, I'm just go do my job, take a few photographs, and come back home," replied Abram.

They all walked into the lights of tall buildings appreciating the night air.

That morning, the next same morning after, after the fall of desperation Craig thought of waiting. He tightened his collars of his long coat as he watched the friends leave the building very early that morning. Stepping over the cold concrete ground he prepared himself for a forced entry into the New Opera Theatre. From the shadows Craig walked over to the side door of the theatre and invited a jack handle to break the lock. He shook the doors once the chain had broken free to walk into the theatre.

Craig following his hunger to eat had not realized that the alarm would sound, and as sure as he wasn't the alarm sounded. Leaving the sound howling through the air of Moscow, and resonating through his cochleae, Craig ran out of the theatre and towards the metro through Pushkin Square. Jumping past people, knocking them into each other, he didn't care but run. Six people watched him rush and others moved when they saw him coming with pace.

"Can't be?! Can't be?! I'm going crazy, you're cool, you're cool, you're cool. I need salt. Can't be?!" cried Craig.

Nudging passed people walking with dogs, and the elderly pouring moonshine to the pavement, he panted and rushed into the metro pushing further people aside. Craig fell into the crowd of morning commuters. He was running from freight as fast as his legs could carry him.

"Whoa, whoa, whoa, move, move!" he began shouting as he heard the train approaching. "Get out my way!" continued to exhale Craig, "Surely I am not crazy."

Twitching his toes, and forcing the patience of people departing the train he looked around to see if he had been followed. The sound seemed natural and there was no movement besides his own thought of ghosts. As Craig panted to catch his breath he entered the train and sat with his hands in his head forcing air to the carriage floor. He began to breathe more easily as he heard the doors close. The train began to rattle the tracks, and he began to rattle his fingers, he looked around slowly steadying himself.

Two silhouettes appeared to notice him as they merged into the background from the next carriage. Craig had not noticed, and this time was too frightened to care that they were not travelling alone. Afraid of his own past he sat in silence for a few stops without motion before leaving the metro and staggering home.

XIII: Math
BLUE

Believing in his passion Tyler dressed in navy and belonged to a political party. This party consisted of his students; they honored him with a blue ribbon. Tyler regarded his students as brothers and sisters and allowed them to bank on him. He had moved from Russia close to Fort Ross, CA, to help all children and also a thousand Muslims in the United States to benefit from the Christian Cross. Moreover from what Tyler had experienced, a wager was to be on balancing Christianity to professional or amateur.

"Bhangra music is fast and upbeat moreover the differences from blues, jazz and bebop music. People of different cultures make the difference in sounds, and balancing the differences is about learning the different types of wave motion," spoke Tyler to his class of physic students. "This is a wave that I'm talking about, and this is a wave to catch your attention."

The class started to laugh as Tyler drew a wave on the board and then waved to the class.

"Sound moves in a wave motion and catches in a medium that waves pass separates the sounds that we hear. Use different lengths of bamboo rods to hear the differing sounds. The wave of a sound will oscillate different to the sounds coming from plucking chords on a banjo or striking keys on a keyboard. We can alter parameters of sounds to achieve a common liking," said Tyler. "AC/DC circuits are measured in waves between voltage and current through a plate of induction. Periodic motion like a spring or a pendulum can be represented as waves to measure forces they exhibit. And as we stated earlier there also exists electromagnetic waves."

"The distance between peaks of a wave is the wavelength. The height of the wave is the amplitude. The time of one repeating segment of a wave is the period, and the number of periods in a second is the frequency. So if I speak really slowly and with depth of base, the frequency will be lower than if I make a squeak for the same second," Tyler gave an example of bass and squeak. "The velocity of that sound is measured by multiplying the frequency with the wavelength. This is measured in meters per second, and famously the equation for the speed of sound in air all relates to the temperature of where the sound is being made. '$V = 331 \text{m/s} + 0.6T_c$.'"

Tyler pressed play on a stereo he had brought. The beat from the box filled the students with energy. They began listening to the music as Tyler presented some questions on the board.

"Bats have an audible hearing of sound that is supersonic, i.e. faster than sound frequencies that we can hear. And they project the sound which is reflected back off surfaces with an increased frequency and above human hearing."

"Sir, can they hear sound from us?" brightly asked one student.

"Hmm, that's a critical question. Unless they are sounding clicks and squeaks of their own as a form of Braille to distinguish us from food or a threat," replied Tyler. "Human hearing is audible not sonic, between 20 – 20,000 Hz in frequency. Okay try these questions with Om in mind to filter out the sound from the beat box, of course," Tyler bopped his head to the beat.

The beacons from his students began to light as they came to the end of answering the questions. Then as the bell bellowed Tyler said: "Ok, class tomorrow we will discuss how brave Will Smith, in 'Independence Day' was by calculating the flight pattern between the gravitational forces of earth and the alien mother-ship, using Kepler's Laws of Planetary Motion, Newton's Law of Universal Gravitation, and the Cavandish Balance Experiment, remember to bring in the brains."

XIV: Math
BLUE

Aware that the post would arrive in the next day or so, and before trying to make himself anymore bluer, Tyler made his best friend aware that he will be moving far away. Tyler sat calmly on the Arbatsko-Pokrovskaya metro-line after wishing his family farewell. He tightened his navy blue bandana and sat thinking on how Derrick would respond to his request.

"I need a lift. More like I'll like a lift so that way you get to see where I'll be living," asked Tyler to Derrick at Venezia Restaurant.

"What you talking about?" asked Derrick.

"Well how can I place this in the words that you will understand? Like a Great Blue Heron, I need to lift off against the centripetal force of gravity '$F_c = mv^2/R$' away from the centripetal acceleration of gravity '$a_c = v^2/R$' to travel at a tangent away from the center of this circle at a certain velocity '$v = 2 \pi R /T$' so I can reach San Francisco by dusk tonight," insisted Tyler.

"Why do you have to go to San Francisco?" asked Derrick.

"I have brought the coordinates for a safe arrival by the board walk. Magnitude and direction for the T.M. torque perpendicular to the earth's center axis that's if we leave now. As after we'll be out of time from the rush of the parade that is about to start there. I promise I'll explain everything to you once we are there," Tyler bravely approached Derrick and whispered slowly, "my friend I have a job opportunity that I cannot miss in California, I hate to leave you more than Moscow, but come with me on this flight so you can always find me."

Derrick did not reply to Tyler's request immediately. Instead he walked with Tyler back to his home. Once they were inside the basement of the theatre, and once Derrick had time to think, he said: "Place some music on and weigh your bag, I'll be out in a minute," basically said Derrick.

Light can be interfaced constructively or destructively. Constructive interference would make light waves bigger in phase and destructive interference would cancel out phases. Digital wave optics allows digital discs to work. Light is bent around corners through slits in a linear media that combine to read encryptions on a digital medium. Infrared light has longer wavelengths that can be bent through interferences that resolve diffractions from compact discs, hence to catch sound on circuit boards. For Young this was second nature to putting sunglasses on.

61

Arriving beside a balustrade facing the Pacific Ocean, just before noon on the same day that they had left, Tyler slowly let go of Derrick. They had arrived on the balcony of where Tyler was to live away from home. From where the friends stood they could see Oakland Bay Bridge, and the greatest deep blue ocean.

"Not bad Tee. Not bad at all," said Derrick.

"There are some binoculars on that barrel there, have a look around," insisted Tyler. "Look at the barquentine boats on the bright ocean surface whilst I get us a few beers."

Geometric optics consists of light that can be refracted, reflected or diffracted. Binoculars are an excellent way of refracting light through a serious of lenses, convex, concave, and plain that allow distant objects to be seen closely and with better resolution. Using lenses to focus light to a different point allowed Galileo Galilei to distinguish parts of the universe. Later out of the blue, Snell's Law brilliantly described how light was used to value diamonds. Measuring the level of bevels to allow refractions of light to become total internal reflections make the diamond more valuable, i.e. the diamond shines light that much more brightly.

XV: Math
BLUE

"**B**alloons form static when rubbed on fabric surfaces. The electrons from the surface that a balloon has rubbed on become attached to the balloon, and then these electrons help the balloon to stick to other surfaces like a wall. Until the balloon loses the attached electrons to equilibrium with the new surface the balloon stays attached," said Tyler to his students in the laboratory of Abraham Lincoln High School, California.

Electrons are charged particles around a nucleus of an atom balancing in space. These particles bring a charge of negativity when spinning around a more positively charged nucleus. Each element has its own specific number of electrons in balance with the number of protons within the nucleus of an atom. Enabling the direction and type of spin of each electron in an atom, agreeing with the weight of the particle as it spins to hold a compound together, that equations were fabricated to carry the integrations into a value. A database of values summing a particular equation of the movement of electrons in space for a desired piece of matter, and possibly cabling that believable sum of energy into an electromagnetic wave, to bring the compound to move from A to B was an achievable hobby. The problem of moving the matter of electrons through other electrons was simple when delivered through space as light, but harnessing the light to travel through the earth's atmosphere in an equation of electrons would prove difficult.

"Basically the light over our heads is delivered through AC circuits. Which means electricity that is traveling back and forth from an alternator or generating transmitter, through power lines across a power grid, to a rectifier that converts the alternating current 'AC,' to a direct current 'DC,' through a switch system, and then back out to the power grid through an inverter," carried on Tyler whilst drawing a diagram explaining the example. "Copper metal conducts electricity the best as their electrons are more close together than any other metallic element on earth. Hence we use copper cords when transmitting current as voltage between car batteries. The thicker the cord the faster the battery will charge."

"Blindingly amazing that a French man and an English man worked together to make the AC/DC reality possible, this happened in 1881. Batteries were being worked on before this by Volta in 1800. The use of a serious of electrolyte half cells when joined with a copper wire increased the heat of an experiment during a lightning storm. The storm must have shocked Volta to think on how to harness that energy. So from the recorded 50 volts between a series of electrolyte cages we have simplified voltage to a comfortable 9 volts for most batteries, a reaction generating heat."

Tyler began to hand out circuit boards to his class. These boards were not at all like conventional boards seen for use by most students in schools. They appeared to be parts of track used to model a speed race course for toy race cars. The men in the room had become overly excited and tried to bear their interest amongst the ladies. Nevertheless the girls had realized that the boys had belayed their attention towards the teacher and thought they too would join in.

"Join the tables together and the track pieces all as one, mount the bulbs on the circuit wherever you like, and once you have done that grab the stools and sit around the track. The red car is for the girls, and the blue car is for the boys," encouraged Tyler.

"Now we shall use the alternating current to provide a direct current through this experiment as I wish to charge the capacitors for future use. The stored capacitance charge is measured in farads 'C = Q/V,' where Q is the charge of an electron. 'R = V/I' meaning the voltage equals current multiplied by resistance. The resistor of the circuit is the cars' measured in ohms, the current is applied through our grid measured in amperes, and the voltage is what's carried in the current and measured as volts," Tyler said as his class worked on the track.

"Okay ladies and gentlemen, each car will travel at the same power in watts '$P = I^2R$' for example, and for emphasis I have not added any inductors or transformers in the circuit so you cannot blame the equipment if things turn blue for either team." Tyler smiled to see his class stare at him. "The overall voltage remains the same for each team which is what?"

"110 volts!" said one of his students and looked out to the class, "Eagle!"

"Excellent! You can give the count."

"I'd like Christina to give the count if that's alright?" Tyler's student replied.

"Sure I'll do it," quickly replied Christina off the mark.

She stood up and walked across to Mr. Hussain. She rattled her bangles and said:

"On the third beep, Ladies ready? Gentlemen ready? Beep, beep, Beep!"

The cars began whizzing around the track and the students encouraged their team car. As the students enjoyed themselves racing each other on and off the track, Tyler wrote their homework for their pass time at home.

"Slowly, slowly, steady, right, right, make it to the home stretch!" cheered a member of the blue team.

Electrical charge 'q' is measured as Coulombs 'C' found by Benjamin Franklin, by the result of rubbing glass and rubber rods with silk and fur cloths. This formed positive and negative charges respectively on the rods. He concluded that "like charges repel and unlike charges attract" as the First Law of Electrostatics states. The Conservation of Energy law states "energy cannot be created or destroyed, but only transferred from one object to another." Thus the energy needed to move an electron is only 1.6×10^{-19} Joules, hardly noticeable that anything just happened, however something just did and that electron is now elsewhere. These statements later used under Coulomb's Law, demonstrated how to find precise forces to move minute masses of positive and negative charges. These charges are generated through turbines of power stations to direct electromagnetic energy to satellites in space or across power grids in our environment.

XVI: Math
BLUE

Praying by staring to the blue sky Derrick immediately became aware that the move for Tyler was a good one. Oblivious to the time Tyler had left to get beers, Derrick made himself comfortable on a deckchair accompanying Tyler's balcony. Like Bill Murray, in 'Lost in Translation,' Derrick drifted into peace amongst the soft sweet scent coming from the ocean.

Having a habit for science Derrick began to place numerals to his surroundings. As a barometer he began calculating the density of the ocean against the earth's atmospheric pressure of 1.01×10^5 Pascal. This was by far an enjoyment factor for him, as he knew the pressure of water in an open environment would equal the force of pressure acting upon it. The pressure is the same as that of the atmosphere. Thus if a boat needs to float then using Archimedes's Principle, the buoyancy would equal the weight of the displaced fluid. Hence dense boats measured by mass/volume, should have enough surface area to displace enough water so the pressure in the ocean can keep the boat afloat in relation to the pressure of the atmosphere.

"Call the doctor when in trouble! Call the doctor when in trouble! Call the doctor when in trouble or when someone falls down. What? They fell over. What? They fell over. What they fell down by the phone box that's burgundy!" sang Derrick hearing Tyler arrive.

"You looking comfortable there, what were you thinking?" Tyler said.

"Well considering you asked. If I can change the magnetic field that is radiated across that channel along the bridge, using Faraday's Law of Electromotive force, 'EMF (V) = - $N\Delta\phi_B/\Delta t$,' and the use of ferromagnetic materials in the surroundings as a magnet, I would be able to create a vacuum large enough to lift the water off the bottom of the sea as Moses did to the River Jordan and walk to the other side," spoke Derrick with a smooth smile as he knew Tyler understood him.

"That would cause way too much radiation to be scattered," encouraged Tyler.

"Beforehand, I would require a bolometer to measure the heat radiation to make sure no bolts or bones are affected along this coast."

"I see. Well when you're done put away your battle bayonets and let's walk down to the peer, see who we find at the parade's bazaar. Now I'm handing you a drink, there's a little alcohol in it, plus there's some ice cubes, no need to figure any effects of thermodynamics or conservation of energy with heat from the scotch. No changing the latent heats of fusion or vaporization, just drink up."

"Ah the old specific heat capacity of a material trick. Heat gained by the ice is heat lost by the drink, and all heat is phased into my belly, and out through my pores. Why do we drink again?"

"To enjoy a little of life my friend," said Tyler. "Stop falling asleep and go take a shower. Need you to look sharp if I'm hoping to boil with someone tonight. However if I consume 1 liter of soda with n amount of moles, within my internal atmospheric pressure of 3 Pa, and being warm interiorly at 20°C, and you not changing the ideal gas constant, using '$PV = nRT$,' what mass of gas will I have by the end of the night?"

Both friends started laughing, not because the joke was funny but because they were both finding an accurate answer. They thought about placing the liquor in the refrigerator and saving the good blue label for later. After they dressed to impress, the scientists staggered beneath the blue sky to San Francisco bay.

XVII: Math
BLUE

"Using a Beaufort scale to measure wind 10 meters off the ground, I have analyzed that we will be having light winds next week, compared to those units expressing a hurricane," said Tyler. "This means that all of you should have your parent's authorization for me to take you to the billiard house next Friday to study momentum and vectors."

Tyler always kept his class enthusiastic about physics, and using real life examples his class achieved brilliant grades with improving accuracy and neatness. Billiards provided a great example to teach them about scalar units, (one number to describe magnitudes, such as mass, temperature, time, etc), vector units, (three numbers to describe magnitude and direction, such as position, velocity, and force), and tensor units, (more than three numbers, such as those to describe a matrix of elasticity).

Upon arriving to the billiard room, Tyler handed them outlines of his teaching. Newton's Law of Motion was to be discussed.

"Newton's First Law," he said. "'Objects at rest remain at rest, and objects in motion remain in a uniform motion unless acted on by an external force.' As you can see the balls will not move unless we strike them, and when we do they'll move uniform to the force that we apply." He raised his cue and tapped a ball to roll. "Newton's Second Law: 'the force applied is equal to the mass of the object multiplied by the acceleration exerted upon it'. Thus I would not need to apply an exceedingly strong force to have this mass move to the pocket way over there."

The class stood in bewilderment to try and understand why Tyler could not explain that at school. At the present time, the class would not have appreciated the external example, but they later would learn to associate grounds on believing the simplicity of Sir Isaac Newton's practices.

"Just like how a rocket needs to have enough force to lift its weight from the ground so do the balls need to move. This is where Newton's Third Law comes into play, 'for every action, there is an equal and opposite reaction,' does anyone understand what I mean?" he asked his students.

No one replied as they were afraid to be wrong outside their common habitat of the classroom.

"Well as you will see in your handouts, acceleration is replaced with the letter 'g' meaning the rocket will have to overcome earth's gravity to lift the mass. The acceleration of gravity is 9.8 m/s^2. Now it's just a simple matter of multiplying mass with 'g' to find the force 'Newtons – kg/m/s' needed," he paused and some students sniffed to show that they understood. "Force equals mass multiplied by velocity or acceleration of gravity 'F = mv or F = mg' depending upon the question."

"Using vectors we can calculate the beauty of trajectory, standstill and the position of landing of that object over there. I don't want any of you to throw the balls at each other but practice the degrees of linear force exhibited when making these billiard balls collide. Do we need exponential forces to move the same mass a longer distance when both masses are the same? Record results on the table I have provided as ticks and crosses for the given experiments."

"Okay class, imagine that these balls are not balls but planets set in space in order to collide. Remembering that energy is conserved from one form to another, we can relate these to momentum. The force of the impact left after a collision can be measured to discover who's to blame."

Tyler continued: "The force of each body is taken into account before and after the collision; '$m_1 v_{1o} + m_2 v_{2o} = m_1 v_{1f} + m_2 v_{2f}$.' The changes in velocity between objects can be evaluated. For instance a 53' Rig hitting a Mini Cooper; the Mini Cooper against the force of the truck will crumble and if the velocity of the truck had not changed, then someone will be out of the job."

The class sniffed softly to hear more.

"The table below the diagram on the next page illustrates using equations how to find the missing factor to objects set in motion. For instance the final velocity of an object when missing the distance traveled in time, the final distance of an object when missing acceleration or final velocity, and the final velocity of object when missing time. All these equations have been rearranged from the simple equations relating velocity 'v,' with distance 's,' time 't,' and acceleration 'a,' to '$v_{avg} = \Delta s/\Delta t$' and '$a_{avg} = \Delta v/\Delta t$.'"

The students began to look uneasy because they were losing all blood to their brains. Seeing them turn colour Tyler asked them to breathe easy as all the equations were a matter of practice. He smiled to reassure his class and allowed them to take a break from understanding Newton's Laws. He prepared their potential energy by running through a few examples on tackling vector quantities; he later packed up the billiard balls, and decided to balance their moods by taking them out for bulk burgers and beverages, in an atmosphere that they enjoyed.

XVIII: Library
BLACK

In the lightly lit central nave of the library of Lomonosov Moscow State University, Derrick sat with Abram and Tyler. From the presence and appearance of these friends they were given silence around their table, that to say that not even the people around them would be smart enough to listen into their conversation. They together were adjusting their thoughts on what they had observed from the broken lock from the morning before.

"Dee and I followed him home. He lives off Begovaya Metro, seems like he lives alone. We watched him enter his home and with lights on we didn't notice any other people or movement besides those that came from him. We could wait in hiding tonight to see if he approaches the theatre and try to make himself vulnerable for exposure?" filled Tyler for Abram.

"That will not be necessary. I'm sure we can keep an eye on him; however what must have possessed him to try and brake into a theatre? Maybe because he had seen Abram and I unloading the equipment the night before the lock was broken? He must have had no idea what to have expected and hence I think he will arrive back soon to find out actually what he saw," anointed Derrick. "We should try and bring him in to make sure he doesn't go too crazy or bring unwanted attention."

"Shall we wait to see if he makes himself known or shall we pull him in? He doesn't seem like the person to bring up a struggle, but I'll take Abram with me just in case," volunteered Tyler.

The library remained busy during the entire day. The place of study was occupied by graduates, students, faculty members of the university and to the public. The library was used to sponsor human resources for individuals that loved to learn or needed a place to find answers. The main building of the university housed the library. During the reign of Stalin, seven neoclassical buildings were constructed around Moscow, where the largest was made into Moscow State University in 1755.

Main metro stations around the facility were Okhotny Ryad and Biblioteka Lenina. M.S.U. founded shopping centers, restaurants, bars, more dining areas, nurseries, classrooms, lecture halls, a bomb shelter, and laboratories to analyze the universities special interest, soil sciences and geology. In the southwest corner of Moscow the building was refurbished modern in 1953 and holds the largest library (according to the number of books) in Russia. The library life focuses on encyclopedic learning for all education specialties.

"Come to think about this, bring him in tomorrow, here. Same time, I'll be here, take Abram to join you. I need to see him up close. I need to know what he saw and analyze if he can be trusted. He can see what we choose for him to see now, nothing besides what we desire, however as far as I can tell, he's an honest man that is short on food, money and love. Possibly we could strengthen our faith by helping him," he said.

"I think you're right. I rather get to meet him and judge his behavior than wait for him to do something stupid. Finding answers about why he was trying to break in will be best delivered from the horse's mouth than us assuming. I will feed him some money or pizza. See which one he responds to better before I bring him to meet you here. Now are you sure a stranger can be trusted?" asked Tyler.

"Oh trust me, checking theories he definitely needs us, without us he will be alone until he dies, and everything that I have predicted to change will not occur without him. Maybe it was his stupidity, his poverty or his curiosity that would kill cats. Nonetheless I need to see him, so don't take no for an answer. And yes feed him before meeting here tomorrow, something light and simple like a coffee and a biscuit to keep him alert," gently spoke Derrick to Tyler and Abram in the quietness of the library.

XIX: Library
BLACK

W ooden bookshelves, tall wooden tables, wooden chairs with padding, along with dark wooden floor board, concrete walls with darkened concrete ceilings covered by wooden beams, and soft lighting kept the library masqueraded with silence over wisdom.

So three times over Derrick read his material to the end of each sentence, paragraph, chapter or book as he learnt from his work. Between sentences he would try not to become distracted by the ladies who tried to acquire his attention as they walked around him. He didn't look around whilst he was in the middle of a sentence. Words he did not recognize he filled with the phrase 'something' and finished his sentences. He would wait till he reached the end of a sentence before sitting back and taking a breather. He had no interest in noticing other people and become distracted from his thought, unless he was observing what would look nice on Tamana or himself. Derrick concluded his work by twirling his pen or tapping the table. He read his work a minimum of three times over to the last sentence to provide himself a mean eighty-five percent accuracy for his decisions every time.

Ninety-five percent averages were what he scored during his tests when he was studying with the faculty of physics and material science at M.S.U. Derrick would give himself a week before his exams to read the material. The first time over to the last sentence would take four days due to understanding both appearance and message of the material. The second time would take him two days. And the third time would take a day to complete to the last sentence. Any other time after that he would just touch the notes and by touch would realize and revise what had been learnt. He had mastered this to reading nine hours one day, three hours the next and twice on the third day, leaving two days to exercise and the last to place the icing. His strategy worked to provide him with a social life alongside.

That social life was spent on his own passions. Together with observing if the girls in the library were observing what other girls were wearing. With Tamana taking pride in her appearance he noticed that she was the girl for him. Tamana made extra effort to look presentable as she believed psychically that this improved health, not only for herself, but also for others around her. She brightened the day for everyone when she came to study. Most the times Derrick was in the library without her, especially after they had graduated. Tamana worked at the medical centre and Derrick worked on his projects.

For company in the times of solitary, Derrick would place invisible insects as spiders and male ladybugs on the table to motivate his mental synapses to fire. He would pretend that they would walk to the shaded areas of the table and wait to either eat or be eaten. Smiling he would finish writing or reading his sentences. If he made a mistake he would simply cross it out with one line and carry on. No white out, nor scribbling in, no more tablets of stone, and no more papyrus to be written on, just simple black ink on paper, leaving the rest of time to hypothesize.

XX: Library
BLACK

The clock had just past three in the afternoon. Derrick was at the library waiting for Abram and Tyler to bring their guest. He was reading a large book with small font up close when he felt the environment change around him. Derrick switched hand of the book which he was reading vertically upwards and turned the page. As the book was large his hands would become tired but not the thirst of his interest. When he realized he was not reading to script but through script as well, he found this to be cool and strong, so he carried on to read for leisure vertically and for information horizontally.

As Derrick turned the next page of his book the light around his table weakened. Tyler and Abram blocked most of the light as they approached Derrick reading. Derrick carried on reading to finish his paragraph before looking up to see their new guest.

"You will not believe where we found him? He was waiting outside the theatre when I went to open the doors for the staff early this morning," Tyler said as he approached Derrick in the library at M.S.U. "Sit down Craig," Tyler said to their new guest. "This is Derrick Tarasov."

Craig sat opposite Derrick with Tyler and Abram sat around the table from him.

"Have you had something to eat?" asked Derrick to Craig.

"Yes, this guy insisted I eat before meeting you. Thank you," replied Craig.

"I know your name, I know where you live, I know that you are living on peanuts, and I know that you tried to break into my theatre a few nights ago. I know all this as that is my work, what I don't know is why you tried to break in?" enquired Derrick.

There was a silence around the table as Derrick waited for an answer.

Craig sniffed a sign of acceptance and said: "I saw you, and this big fellow, emptying a van in the middle of the night the day before I broke in. I was looking to steal from you. I'm sorry. I am truly sorry. Please I'll do anything you ask of me, just don't have me arrested. I suffer from Parkinson's and the law cannot understand. Help me."

"Help you? Like how?" asked Tyler.

"You will never believe me, but I was waiting for you earlier today as I'm sure you would be able to explain what I saw at your place."

The three friends waited for Craig to continue with what he was stuttering to say.

"I saw me, I saw me, there on the other side of your door. I saw me looking straight at me, wearing the same clothes that I had on that night. He smiled at me, and with freight I stood for a moment and bells starting to ring, that is when I fled instead of falling to the floor. I ran. I ran home thinking I may have imagined that. These past days I thought that it was a mirror I had seen my reflection in," Craig paused. "But I asked myself to leave. And now I think I'm going crazy."

Craig sat staring at Derrick, he glanced at Tyler and then to Abram. Abram bowed his sight to the table. Craig did the same.

"You realize I lost everything from your greed. My theatre was in ruins after the last incident. A wreckage was made but you are not well aware of that. Nevertheless you are showing great mercy now, and that through the hand that you dealt, I am with great gratitude for whatever made it possible for you to meet me," said Derrick. "I need something from you."

"Anything, however I have nothing to offer you except myself, but please explain to me what I saw. I cannot sleep, work, or even breathe without sweating. I will do anything you ask me. Was what I saw a reflection? Then again how can a reflection speak back? I'm a good man. I'm a good man. I'm a good man. What would you like from me? Don't report me to the police, I have nothing of yours."

Derrick leaned over the table and brought his hands together. Tightening his grip with both hands he expanded them out like he was holding a world of knowledge between them. Moving his fingertips as some sort of chart mapping he organized his archive of thought within the sphere of perplexes. Derrick sat for several moments in his own world with his friends around him. He pitched and forked ideas of progression within the space of his hands. The rhythm of Derrick's thought was felt by his friends and Craig. Slowly the rhythm slowed; sliding his palms over each other he made contact with his smallest fingers and brought his thought back to rest. Derrick tapped his index fingers together and began playing incy-wincy spider with his fingers.

"Go home, wear the same clothes you had on two nights ago, and meet me tonight at the theatre. Come and speak to Abram, this big fellow," Derrick said looking at Craig and gesturing over to Abram. "Meet me tonight after nine; make sure you are wearing the same clothes. I assure you there is nothing to be concerned about; I am not calling any authorities on you. Let's say I need you to help as a backstage extra," Derrick said as he sat back and looked towards the library's exit. "I appreciate your confession Craig."

Whilst bowed to the table Craig said before leaving, "I appreciate your forgiveness Derrick."

XXI: Relations
GREEN

Gradually coming to an understanding about how men and women can stand together goes a long way as communion of grass blades growing. Meaning there are as many men and women as there are grass blades standing together, then stems grow, and later trees with leaves, and with ivy vines to blooming apples and pears. Some like to try herbs as coriander, parsley, and basil before planting anything firm whilst others like to see if they would like to add chilies, jalapeños and certain capsicums with their diet.

The guys had a system to prepare themselves on finding the right caterpillar. The guys would circulate three dates a month whilst in education and kept this rhythm occurring until they graduated. Later they would intend to circle the globe, arrive back home, enter employment and decide to love old grapes or pick new ones. As for Derrick he allowed his caterpillar to grow, cocoon, to hatch from the chrysalis and into adult Tamana.

Grounds for the strategy would not have started during freshman year. Freshman year was used to make friends and find common interest with new colleagues during education. The friends agreed on a strong foundation with their peers, for themselves, and for each other as they progressed into adulthood.

Within the woods of the parks that they were near they would meet after school during their adolescent years. Here they would discuss on how to introduce themselves to the opposite sex. They sat amongst the trunks of trees and themselves around a campfire. As the ground warmed around them the crickets began to click.

They pitched ideas on settling on an agreement for maintaining a three date average a month. The guys loved their work but they needed to understand what love was elsewhere. Luscious appearances of multi-desires all need to be loved as particularly admiring a certain somebody can be hard to judge. As sparrows listening over each other the guys spoke in third dialect within each other's speeches, mastering how love in friendship can co-exist with love for another.

So they laughed whilst throwing sandal wood chippings into the fire, and the fire roared upon combustion to help keep them warm. In the quietness of the forest a hard crackling came loud and with a thud. A log of lumber landed in front of them from tumbling down to gravity from the branches high above. Their decision was made when the natural plank of wood covered with fur and moss landed between them and the fire.

They concluded by their lives being spared that their decision towards finding true love by statistical assortment from a random population was a good one.

XXII: Relations
GREEN

Grace was delivered into dining for the first date for all the guys. For all people over all the metro lines to affordable restaurants and cafes scattered along Zamoskvoretskaya Metro. The truth for the friends to take their first dates out dining on the last Friday of the first month of graduate school allowed them to assess their date.

Eating food from salads with crisphead, romaine, butterhead, or other leaf varieties of lettuce to a little meat on the side, and other members of vegetables as green beans to a little dressing and some drink, wine or not, allowed the conversations made to sound in scrumptious expression.

If the date wasn't going well then there was always the food to adore. Later leaving a peaceful peck on the cheek by the bus or metro stop, or at their date's front door enabled them to move onto the next date. The guys would usually meet one or another at the local twenty-four hour fast food diner, mostly Sbarro Pizza, to discuss some fun or why they weren't invited through the gate.

Dining included times that were juggled around study. Sometimes dining with a date had to be forced into lunch times or quick breaks between lectures. The men from the friends happened not to waste time when deciding to approach the women. They approached women they found attractive when they felt they needed to express their feelings for them. Mostly the social networking was performed by trial and error. Libraries were used to study just as breaks were used for coffee.

Tyler would take out girls he fancied due to their charismas for Starbucks during lunch. He would watch them buy a muffin and then he would allow them to watch him place his money back in his pocket. A gracious smile was what he watched for, plus he waited to watch if she noticed other girls. Like Abram and Derrick they only dated girls that had girlfriends.

Girls that were suited to see what other girls were wearing led themselves into further dates. Sometimes the second date in the second month would lead to a third date in the third month, but never would there be an intimate relationship before graduating. Dining more than once a month with the same girl depended upon the grandeur of their work and the grace of their date.

Tamana had a predisposition of facial symmetry with most her dates. That to mean she would screw-up her face when she felt uncomfortable, showing a face of anger and disgust if she felt threatened. She had learnt that scrolling her fingers would work to defend her position. Furthermore she developed the ability not be embarrassed in public. The guys she dated quickly learnt that about her, that to just hold open a door for Tamana would be considered as strong as a date. The second date would be her bumping into you whereas the third date would be to break.

To be born in right proportions as intended through Adam and Eve allowed most to become envious. Gleeful covered girls with modest guys that were not in pray came to realize that God had other intentions. Through freight, crime, greenery amongst the same or crossing genders, would have brought smiling towards personal shopping fears for genocide. Into the darkness like disability they can enjoy forever. That was another reason the guys dated on a gradient as through this gradient they gave to others.

XXIII: Relations
GREEN

Sitting with Tamana in Sbarro Restaurant, in their favorite location next to the jungle painted wall she asked Abram for some advice.

"I have nothing to talk about when I'm on a date. What do you guys talk about? And what do the girls you date talk about? I'm losing my mind; I keep thinking about talking to the guys I'm with about medicine, pharmacy crosses, or gangrene," asked Tamana.

Abram laughed, gave a sigh and said: "That's funny. Well you are half on the right track. Listen to this story: Shree Krishna, 'The Lord in Hindu scripture that agreed with Prophet Prince Arjun, that his salvation was made regardless that he killed his brother or not. Lord Krishna was a friend of Arjun's, and was his charioteer in the Kuruksetra War, 5000 B.C.' Now before this, gopies were all the farm girls, all girls loved Lord Krishna, not because He was from God, but was God Himself for the people. So the girls' flirted their good stuff amongst Him to grab His attention. He gowned them clothes in all colours to try to keep something on them. Now these gopies only had questions to ask Him. Then there came one girl that He found fond liking as she studied in various arts and spoke of her interests, and asked Shree Krishna of His. So you can either ask questions to your dates or find more things that interest you and talk about them. Possibly give time to listen to your date. Ask him what he likes to be worn on a woman. Share some interests of his. Overall enjoy time away from work. Show confidence to other girls around you if you cannot find any common ground with your date."

"Like, what are you doing tonight? Or, I like to do my nails."

"That's good, that's more like it. Now if I wish to pick up on the nails thing I can but it's second date night tonight, so hate to leave you but I have to glide out of here."

Second date night for Tamana was usually non-existent. She had feelings for Derrick since youth and rarely allowed a date to reach the second month. Nevertheless she felt at times a second date was needed, times when she wished to make a point, or times when an Antonio Banderas would have bumped past her with grace and asked with sincerity for the time to be spent with her. These dates after dining would follow into the cinemas or dancing with a dark green bottle of Carlsburg by her girlfriends and Banderas.

The guys happened to help each other on the second dates. They would join a night for the second date qualifiers at Brunswick Bowling Lanes. They would wait for each other and their dates at Shosse Entuziastov Metro, on a Friday or Sunday, to walk to the bowling alley. Cans of Sprite or 7-Up, if so Mountain Dew, maybe with water or vodka, great for the guys as they would warm the girls, and great for the girls as they would warm each other. Neon lighting with twelve pound bottle green bowling balls kept the men shooting turkeys well past graduation.

XXIV: Relations
GREEN

Camouflaged within the shades of leaves their clothes completely made them invisible amongst their surroundings. Through having darkened paint smeared across their faces, only the white of their teeth and corneas could be seen. The beasts in the jungle knew of their presence, the birds watched with stealth themselves, and both stayed silent not to give the commandos colours away.

In solitary these men have lived without any pleasures from women. Days, to weeks, to months, to years had passed since they had set up camp in the middle of the Amazon. They silently stand in secret away from the working world. They remain concealed away from humanity. The light that they share shines in from the sunlight in the day between branches of leaves and lanterns from locals during the night.

The ground would shake to make the trees drop fruits for them. Currently they remain waiting for the world's leaders to destroy each other. Grace fall onto my unborn child, the g-chord would ring, and they will be able to raise humanity once again, simply because they showed love.

Nothing was past their tendency for their passion for what they knew to exist. They glowed with radiance together as they knew how to show love. Times amongst cries could be heard through the night carried by howling of the wind. They would look left on their own trunk to bring to reason their existence to live.

Gravitopism would enable them not to fall over, and phototropism would enable them to grow towards the light. However at times with closer observation they could be seen bending their bark to peer their appendages through residential windows, or imitate curves of gravel lining roads.

The earth had yielded a fine group of soldiers. They showed love unlike those that had plenty of green from the sweat of making others cry. These men adapted well in their chlorophyll filled leaves and cellulose based cell walls. They were the most merciful. There was no one stronger. Glad to say that they were the only ones worthy enough to live on this globe.

XXV: Relations
GREEN

"That glitter dress would look nice on you. That velvet dress would look nice on you. That dress would look nice on you. This would look nice on you. These would look nice on you. Those combat pants would look nice on you. That Brazil t-shirt would look nice on you. She would look nice on you, these would look nice on you and this would look nice on me, Score!" said Derrick as he walked with Tamana on their third date around Okhotny Ryad Shopping Centre.

"If you like it, like seriously like it, then I'll buy it," she said.

"Well make sure to try it on first. Besides I like video games, Grand Theft Auto is a cool game, Halo is a cool game, Pro-Evolution Soccer is a cool game, Need for Speed-Most Wanted, is a cool game, Tekken Tag is a cool game, the Nintendo Wii seems to have cool games, SSX3 is the coolest game, however can you buy some lunch instead?" he asked.

Abram's third date happened to be with a girl whose role model was Beyonce Knowles. He happened to see her in Starbucks whilst he was entertaining another girl. The girl happened to grab his attention by speaking about Cassius Clay during drinking coffee with her friend. Abram smiled over at her to acknowledge he liked her tone of voice. And not being the shy type she slipped Abram her number, time, date, and place for Friday night dancing.

The glorious girl wore clothes that left just enough to the imagination. The secret to her success was to sleep with her mouth open. Along with taking pride in her appearance she practiced the stance of yoga when resting or working. The stance was to maintain first finger and thumb contact to keep her heart beating. Improving cellular metabolism with the heart pulsing kept her in shape. This glorious girl managed to receive a third date, and on this date Abram took her to the zoo.

"I would like to see an Emerald Lizard," mentioned Abram.

"I would like to see the Siberian Tiger," said his date.

"That is a gorgeous animal. Hope he's not sleeping," said Abram.

"I'll wake him with a growl," she said.

"Now that just turned hot into sexy."

"Enough to add me to twice a month?"

"Hey look we're here Barrikadnaya Metro Station. And I'll have to hear that growl before I can decide."

The doorbell rang to Tyler's apartment. His third date was movie night with a choice between watching Gladiator's, Russell Crowe or Gerard Butler's, role in 300. The Gladiator was given more emphasis by his date as there was less gore. Whereas with 300 there was a likely chance that she would end up throwing herself on Tyler.

"I wouldn't mind watching a comedy if you'd prefer?" asked Tyler.

"Action suits me just fine. Do you mind if I take my boots off?" asked his date.

"If you like. That's a nice glittery hijab, how many do you have? And would you like a drink?"

"What do you have? And I have several. My favorite is a white stitched one with lace."

"Beer, wine, apple juice, orange juice, water and milk."

"Do you have any cookies?"

"I have some cookies and cream ice-cream if that's what you were thinking."

"What are you going to have?"

"Mmm…. I'll blend the ice-cream with a little milk and sugar to make a shake."

"Do you have any white wine?" she said and began laughing to herself. "Forget that, I'll have a cold soda if you have one."

Tyler chose the movies to see his date's reaction towards movies of leadership, honor and righteousness, this in all to find grounds for her grace for ending gruesome suffering. His heart filled with love for this girl as she gave a tear gladly to the mercy of the Gladiator.

XXVI: Relations
GREEN

Usually an image of jealousy and envious cruelty projected from the edges away from the surface of emeralds. A decision was made by noble persons to have all things flicked off to be adjusted to mark churchmanship. Thus gothic graves were turned to greased gears that peddled gondolas across sea water as grasshoppers across lawns.

"Managed to find yourself to me this time? What have you come to let me know? That my time is still yet to come? How can you judge your time around me? What if I was sitting there?" asked Craig. "Yes, you can probably answer all questions, mostly with more reason to persuade yourself other than anyone else."

"One thing I could not predict was your gratitude that you have. What living around all these g-strings you have become an old fart," replied Derrick. "Thought you would be able to handle the sunshine?"

"Get out of here man! There is nothing for you here."

"What? I have come to listen to the music, hear the wave's crash onto the shore, the sweet smell of sea water, the sound of birds in the sky, the sight of bright papayas selling around every corner, ripe coconuts hanging from the palm trees, not your lazy ass. Now take your turn!" demanded Derrick whilst he poured himself a glass of water.

Since his last move Craig had opted to stay in Copacabana Borough. From traveling with the friends that made him a brother, they were not pleased for him to leave them. Nevertheless by the end of 2010, Rio de Janeiro, Brazil, South America had become home to Craig Goncharov. Through the festival that the friends had come to see Craig met Gwyneth and fell in love.

Waiting in line at a local bar across the stretch of Copacabana Beach the friends spoke Russian in Rio. Every other person spoke Portuguese except Gwyneth who spoke both languages freely. The accents changed to find common ground, (that ground found being their tongues), from then Craig remained behind in Brazil as the others waiting for each other to age.

"Teach me what you have learnt in your travels young scholar," asked Craig as he moved his knight three spaces.

"I witnessed the finding of the Holy Grail," Derrick said, and moved his king close to Craig's knight. "Inscription laid out in the mind of a young

101

adult, Thomas Guy, who lived 1645 to 1724, and was a bookseller whom later founded Guy's Hospital of London. Later another fell and broke all boundaries to establish Guy's legacy. The Holy Grail was founded when all men thought on one wavelength. That all men are now bowing over to the Messiah for forgiveness and not to sand on beautiful women."

"So that is true. I had felt much calmer winds living here. There is something of peace written in this so called stranger's testimony that I wish to be worthy to untie his sandals. I mean the personas have begun to speak in a richer dialect. Walking in the market I hear speech expressions on niños have changed. They are actually speaking to the adults, all about a country amigo trabajar as a till clerk silencing the ignorance of Americano pride."

"The truth to the Holy Grail is that no man needs to fall at anyone's feet no longer but that of the Messiah's alone. The new founder insisted to nail Jesus before the wood began to degrade and rot, and the Father watched Him be raised so all could have a chance to see Heaven. Thus I went to seek the birth of trees. Gradually back in time but this gyroscope measured me back to the present all times I registered for Genesis. I know I will not get to see the first man, but I'm sure you'd agree that we should believe in him."

The last words to come out of Craig's mouth before he checkmated Derrick were: "God is Good."

Craig felt greatly overwhelmed to hear Derrick paint that picture for him. Distinct measures of Derrick's vocal pitch turned the world's dark jealousy around them into umbrella cocktails with drops of sour light lime like Lyublinskaya Metro line.

XXVII: Sport
BLACK

"*A grand opening to the massive event of 2008 here in Quebec City. What a glorious start to a hundred year anniversary in International Ice Hockey. Canada with the last win in 2007 on Russian soil, and now for the first time in 100 years Canada is hosting the beginning of another fantastic win against Russia.*"

"*Last year the Canadian national team clenched the title from the Russians, and progressed to beat the awesome Finland team winning the 2007 IIHF title. Can they do the same this year against the mighty Russian squad on home ground?!*"

"*If the passion for Team Canada is as much as the excitement as the crowd brewing here in Colisee Pepsi Arena, then we are in for a fantastic night. Three periods of explosive energy, I just can't contain myself Cephus!*"

"*Amazing absolutely Juan, best to put down the coffee and hold onto your seat. The arena seems to be as excited as we are, the ice is being polished, and looks like the dens are being loaded!*"

Early hours of a morning Craig pulled open the side entrance door to the New Opera Theatre.

"Leave from here Craig. Leave Now!" cried future Craig to his counter self.

Craig made his past self vanish from freight in the matter of seconds without thought. He looked over at Derrick as Derrick walked out of the shadows to pat Craig on the shoulder.

"I almost scared myself," said Craig. "Dam I definitely scared him."

Derrick closed the door and led him inside.

"Hold onto the time-machine once again as we have somewhere to be," asked Derrick. "Take a deep breath."

The room began to chill and crackles of sound formed electrical charge separating the air space around them. Derrick and Craig lost touch of the ground as they became covered in subatomic aura bright enough for them to shut their eyes. A pulse of potential energy released itself from the time-machine and was drawn back as kinetic energy, leaving nothing but naked space in the basement of the New Opera Theatre.

Landing outside the Colisee Pepsi Stadium in Quebec City, Canada, on Sunday May 19th 2008, Derrick and Craig presented themselves between the path of the car park and the stadium. Craig opened his eyes slowly to hear talking from the

105

distance. As much to their surprise they witnessed the Big Red Machine walking from the distance towards them.

"What is the Russian Team doing over there? Shouldn't they be inside?" said Derrick.

He looked over at the main entrance to the stadium and saw the coach for Team Canada. Team Canada was exiting the bus outside the stadium into the building. The Russian team, Big Red Machine, was approaching Derrick and Craig, but with their sight fixed to walk past them. They were uttering abuse amongst each other. Derrick recognized the team captain Alexei Morozov, and approached him.

"Hey Morozov, couldn't you get parking closer to the arena?" he said.

"Don't get me started man. We were also stopped by the Canadian police on our way here, you'd think an international event would host appropriate measures for the teams. Now I'm witnessing the Canadians walking in, and we have been carrying our gear over a kilometer. Seriously man, who are you?" said Morozov.

"Well for Russia, for me, and for my friends you make sure you win tonight. Just be cool and no doubt we'll win. We'll take that title back and on their home ground. Now get to the cloakroom, Oorah! Don't let them get to you. We are here for them, you remember that," said Derrick looking at Morozov, and then the rest of the men.

"Ya, for CSKA Moscow!" shouted Craig.

"For CSKA Moscow!" shouted back the Big Red Machine.

CSKA Moscow stood for Centraliy Sportiviy Klub Armii, which translated to the Army's Central Sport Club. They were the best in the Continental Hockey League and in the European Champions Cup. They dominated the Soviet League for forty-six years winning 32 titles, (and one streak of 13 titles), compared to the closest rivals Montreal Canadiens at 24 titles, (and a streak of five titles). CSKA Moscow was the best at what they did with no team ever to have come close.

Ice hockey was first played indoors in Montreal, at Victoria Skating Rink, on March 3rd 1875. Since then they had climbed to become one of the most talented orientated sports of all time. Cold countries such as Canada, Scandinavia and Russia dominated the recruitment in finding the athletes of this sport. The National Hockey League supported by the American government went to greater lengths to sponsor the life of the sport, and with more indoor arenas the sport has stayed alive for over a century.

From 1946, CSKA Moscow had set the bar and brought the challenge into the sport. Anatoli

Tarasov, played on ice and then coached the team from 1953-1974. After this time the number of players signing for the sport began to decline till 1980 as the Soviet Union changed to the Red Army Team. New players were to be sieved to find the best athletes and them to be shifted for work in the Red Army instead. Thus attributes of CSKA Moscow declined, and the last game played was a friendly with the Russian National Team, Big Red Machine, playing in January 2008.

"Sliding onto the ice the officials have made their way. The teams are all aligned and the puck is about to drop."

"As we count down to a fast paced action packed game I would like to mention the pressure that our visitors are to face. The Russian Machine has not won a title for fifteen years with their last being captained by Vyacheslav Bykov in 1993. Now he's coaching the team to hopefully take the World Championship 2008 title back to Moscow, but can he break the Canadian spirit? The atmosphere of this ice rink makes this extremely hard to imagine!"

"Nevertheless Juan, Bykov has led the team with outstanding outcomes against the Swiss and the Finns to bring them here today. We hope this

game is a clean one, all supporters are to enjoy and there are many supporters in the crowd, a nice clean competition."

"Ha. You're right Cephus; if the heat of this fabulous stadium becomes any warmer we will not have any ice to play on. O.K.... the puck is dropped and possession has immediately fallen to the home team!"

XXVIII: Sport
BLACK

Of a crowd close to the full capacity of fifteen-thousand people, Derrick and Craig made way to find their friends in the arena. Squeezing past French speaking Canadians they climbed down the alley and crossed the right wing opposite the team dens to be welcomed by Tamana, Tyler and Abram. Their view stretched close to a diagonal clockwise of the whole arena.

"What took you so long?" asked Tamana, as she made space for Derrick and Craig to pass. "Your seats were becoming cold." She winked at Craig as she kissed her boyfriend.

"I've got to say that this is by far the coolest atmosphere of hockey that I have ever seen," said Abram.

"By far the coolest Derrick. Can't believe you thought of this night here. Is there something you are not telling us? What year are we in?" asked Tyler. "What happened to watching the game from Khodynka Arena next year? Don't leave us here now Dee, seems like we are a long way from Belorusskaya Metro, and Dee where did I park my car?"

"So are you going to let us know how we got here in the first place?" asked Abram.

"Cephus that was a strong first period. Seems like the home team are showing full devotion for their crowd here in Quebec. Superb having the Big Red Machine fighting for their twenty-fourth title. If they manage to take the title home they will tie with Team Canada on world championship titles. This can be likely as they haven't lost a game this season."

"Yes Juan, I really enjoy watching the officials skate across the ice. Still amazes me how they manage to dodge the biscuit as it flies across, that, and how they manage to keep their distance from the players. I think they should wear more padding."

"Crying out loud Cephus, they are professionals, no need to worry, best for us to stay here and them to be there. I tried skating once, carried on going forward until I hit the wall, then I went the other way until I hit the wall, then I skated back, decided to stop half way through and then I couldn't start again. I was stuck in the middle of the ice until I managed to crawl my way out."

"Excellent Juan. Well... I see that the goal keepers have made their way to the goals and time to begin the second period."

"Simple really Abram. Simple once I figured out what would happen if the earth stopped still. The idea came to me when I saw someone fall off the metro and checked around to see if anyone had noticed. There was no one there besides me, and she never saw that I had noticed. However the lady felt so embarrassed that she started weeping. Then I thought what is she crying for? The earth would still move after we fall into it. As long as the earth keeps on turning the Lord can keep gathering souls to build heaven," returned Derrick. "This got be thinking on how much energy I would need to freeze a tear instantly in a second, in joules."

"The specific heat capacity for grams in seconds, I see where you're heading with that," added Tyler.

Derrick paused for a moment and nodded his head believing Tyler was on the right track.

"So what if the earth stopped turning? Everything would become sucked into the ground including this arena. Not a pleasant thought right?" he continued.

"Oh, so then what?" asked Tamana.

The sound of the game, the shouting of spectators, the chants of the horn, and the whistle of the referees drowned out the conversation that Derrick was having with his friends. In addition the spectators were consumed within the match that they had no interest in anything else.

Derrick spoke the story whilst looking mostly straight across the field of play. Somewhere past the barriers, into the crowd, up a flight of stairs, between a pair of stewards, into a fire exit, he held the world and watched the players' skate above it. He continued in his explanation looking past the people that came from the exit.

"I calculated that if I happened to stop the earth turning for a split moment, I would be able to control where the earth would be when I started the earth turning again. The gradient of the forests work in both directions, but mostly away from the direction of the wind. Then I realized that I could make this easier if I could harness the energy of Reka Moskva and Volga Canal, to use the delta system to triangulate the hold of the earth's gravity."

Derrick looked over at his friends realizing that they didn't understand but were paying full interest not to critique.

"Imagine holding the earth's electromagnetic current from the core of the earth and summing that energy to another point, that point being the sun's hold of the earth. Making this point the South Pole and the North Pole being any time and place I wish. The release of reserved energy would spin a swing shot for the earth around the sun to whenever I like as recoil."

Tamana had studied a little physics and so had Tyler, now however along with Abram they began watching the game as Derrick. The first time Abram and Derrick began to watch a game as such was when Nascar played on television. Being at the racetrack was altogether a different idea, but what was the point of watching cars circle around and around? The point was to hold the background as the camera man changed. And the world that they experienced on HD was worth watching. Like this game, Abram paid attention to the game as Derrick.

"Those boxes that night when you decided to break-in contained uranium crystals. Uranium has four oxidation states and four levels of ionization energies that can be struck to release explosive energy. Abram and I collected them from the geology unit at Lomonosov," Derrick looked over at Abram and said: "If he knew what he was carrying for me he would have charged extra." And stroked his right thigh with his third finger.

"Oh I see why you didn't need any help unpacking them now," replied Abram without turning over to look at Derrick. "Out of 0.05% of the Russian population, that is about 78,000 people that sign up to play hockey a year, we can't find a squad to take the lead in this game."

Derrick smiled and carried on with what he was saying: "Using the uranium and composing them within electrolytic minerals such as sodium

114

cations 'the oxidizing agent' at one end, and sulfur anions on the other 'the reducing agent,' with separate casing cased over with a pure titanium casing, this would allow the minerals to keep their electromagnetic properties as they would have in natural form. The casing of this staff is pretty thin, but the density is extremely great, which keeps the mass of the staff sufficient for the staff to stand straight on gravity. And sheathing the casing within itself I can control the volume to surface area for which the solution can be carried. What that means is that it can be mobile when not on."

"So that was the reason why I couldn't move an inch once you switched the switch and for some moments after I opened my eyes?" rhetorically asked Tyler.

"The possibility of us holding against the acceleration of gravity is impossible to imagine. Imagine we were floating as the earth turned. But somehow we are here and not where we were."

Pausing for a moment to watch Team Canada come two goals ahead of the Russian team, with the Canadians becoming excited around them, Derrick looked over at Abram. Caring for a comfort reason Abram looked over at all the girls. The only reason for what Abram cared about was why Derrick had brought him there? Abram looked around at the Canadian supporters chanting the score in French with excitement.

115

"The Russian Hockey Federation is having a hard time to meet the competition this year. They rank fifth place entering this final event we are having. The best possibility tonight is if they are able to hold that standing. If Ken Hitchcock's team overcomes Vyacheslav Bykov's team tonight then we are in for a celebration."

"Best not to underestimate the Russian team Juan. Trailing two goals with twenty minutes still to play in the third period, I am glad that we are not in Moscow witnessing this event."

"Well, what do we all do when we get knocked down? We pick ourselves back up again!"

"I couldn't agree with you anymore Juan."

"That sounds great Cephus. Well to our audience at home we look forward to seeing you back after this short commercial break."

"Later I triangulated the frame of energy I would need to hold my force on gravity against gravity around Moscow. Moscow is 1,080 kilometers^2, that's 417 miles^2. Not much of a distance compared to the circumference of the earth, however I thought I had to start somewhere. Now using details of my mass multiplied by the acceleration of gravity gave me a force in Newtons. My force was extremely large to the area I was to electro-magnetize, so I used the energy of the moving water in the seas around Russia to

116

extremely, exceedingly, exceptionally reduce my mass allowing me to hover over the turning earth."

"You mean you found the energy it takes to hold the water of the seas to the earth?" enquired Tyler.

Derrick looked at him and blinked: "and adding them together, the Sea of Azov, the Baltic Sea, the Caspian Sea, the White Sea, and the Black Sea to find the pressure they exert around Russia. Surprisingly I realized I could minus the density of the water from the earth's density and have minimum effort with moving the earth alone. Using a spark plug and a magnet the current separates the uranium particles into radicals, and used as massive amounts of energy radiating from the staff cored into itself to hold the earth, and allow the staff to repel and float," Derrick paused with some concern for a second.

He continued: "The first time I thought about flicking the switch I had forgotten to place the time and where to land. Almost blew up the world. If I knew coordinates in space for safe landing I'm sure I would have altered them. Later I calculated that I could travel with my friends as long as I knew how much each of you weighed. Adding insulators as carbon fiber to this device was the last thing. All allowed me to use the force of energy needed to move a mass at the speed of light^2 to follow us here, only $E=mc^2$."

XXIX: Sport
BLACK

"*T*he thighs and the backs of these athletes must be aching to the core. Can only imagine how they are to feel once this night is over.*"

"*This night is still not yet over and these soldiers are not getting paid pennies for their work. We hope to see a fantastic response by the Big Red Machine, and if Hitchcock has told anything to his crew is that they should play this period with caution.*"

"*They are getting paid to touch other men. Let's hope to see a good response.*"

Returning back from bringing snacks from the kiosk the friends sat down with anticipation for their home team to win. Abram's passion towards his faith was about to bring tears into his eyes. To him this wasn't a game, this was really life, and as this was really life he would be in a foul mood all week if his team was to lose.

As for Tyler he enjoyed sports as the next person. Tyler was suited to watch soccer, forty-five minutes one direction without moving his head away from the screen, and forty-five minutes the other. Best to keep all objects away from him in case his team lost or the other team fouled. He found ice hockey difficult to watch on television as the ice blinded his sight; however he still managed to watch some by staring at the black television frame whilst the game played.

As for this game; Tyler and Abram sat close to one another with a tight grip for the other to stay calm. The mercenaries tried not to swear, however after the fourth goal Tyler cried out an insult that shocked the screaming audience around him.

Derrick brought Craig as Craig had no one to enjoy life with. Craig was a man and assuming that any man likes the company of men, that Derrick allowed Craig to enter his circle. Craig enjoyed ice hockey from all other sports. Without a television he caught up with the pucks in play by sitting beside a local barber's radio. Craig instantly loved Derrick as gave Craig purpose.

"Where did that come from? A shred of time into the third period and Russian, Alexei Tershchenko has closed the gap to one behind. Team Canada and Cam Ward did not see that forced entry."

"There is still hope for the team away Cephus. The arena atmosphere has shifted; if the

home supporters don't bring their spirits to the brim then they may be going home with a frown."

"Juan, the gold medal champions from 2007 should be able to hold off the elite pressure of the Russians, we just have to hope that no more mistakes happen. Oh dear! Oh dear! Where did that come from?"

"That came from Ilva Kovalchuk, Kovalchuk has not scored any goals in this championship but has just equalized for the white, blue and red."

"The Canadian goalkeeper Cam Ward is devastated by that outcome."

"How can we blame him? He had no time to even catch his breath before the Russians responded again with the equalizer."

"Shalbu! Shalbu! Shalbu!" cheered Abram.

"Shalbu!" chanted Russian supporters.

"Ah just as great as Viktor Tikhonov," Abram said turning round to look at Derrick.

Viktor Tikhonov, was as famous as Anatoli Tarasov, in CSKA hockey. He played from nineteen to thirty-three, and from thirty-four in 1964 became coach for Dynamo Moscow. Later he seeded Vasily Tikhonov, who seeded Viktor Tikhonov II, who became drafted by NHL Phoenix Coyotes that year, 2008. Derrick realized that Abram was speaking about Viktor Senior.

"Now that's what I'm saying!" said Abram.

"I don't know what you mean Abram, would you like some chips?" asked Derrick as the horn to the end of the third period hollered.

"Can we believe this!? Do we want to believe this!? Can this even be possible!?"

"Three minutes into extra time, and Canadian Rick Nash could not stop the stamina of Kovalchuk forcing the puck over the shoulder of Ward, and through the Canadian net. His soul, his flesh, his will to be remembered forever seemed to be driving him."

"Let's give to Yevgeny Nabokov, the Red Machine goalie for his defense against the pressures of the Canadian squad. The goaltender voted the most fearsome by the Canadians."

"The Russian Team entered the competition in fifth place and now ranks second in the world. Mare ten points shy from the Canadians International Ice Hockey Federation stats as 3400 from 3010. As for 2008 the Russians have tied with 24 titles in IIHF World Championship, alongside Canada. Tonight the Russians conquered Canada with great anger and furious passion."

"And tonight they are going home settling their defeat against the Canadians last year. Marking up before the ice melted they staked the bread before the twig rotted,. 5-4 Russia."

XXX: Nutrition
YELLOW

Yielding to the force of nature Abram exercised daily. Every morning he would wake to watch the daffodils in his vase turn their faces towards the sunlight shining into his apartment in Egypt. Abram had moved to this northern state of Africa as he was appointed by the Chairman of Water, for the African Water Facility, to bring yeoman to the continent. His job was suited to him best as he spoke the Negro language of West Africa, Yoruba, along with Arabic, and Russian.

He practiced yoga each morning before eating healthy amounts of fats and carbohydrates. He would consume a whole melon in the mornings. The fruit would provide him with intrinsic sugars as electrolytes with water that would keep him nourished and hydrated during work. Egypt day was by far a contrast from days in Moscow, so to prevent heatstroke sport drinks were consumed by the liter to keep the synapses firing faster.

Since youth he had used his technique to physically contain his energy balance in a positive manner, i.e. to increase energy intake and reduce energy output. This would allow his basal metabolism to respond much faster, and relax the bodies resting metabolism at a greater rate, just as Yellow Hammers or Japanese Hornets would when resting from motion. A behavior modification from drinking yeast fermenting sugar drinks, into eating low-fat diets with complex carbohydrates with resistant exercise, kept Abram as solid as a steed yoked to a carriage.

From yesteryears the situation that all men had was the yank of tension and this in the heat was that much more uncomfortable. Yahweh brought consciousness into animals but some became confused along the way. Young, to youngsters, to yashmaks allowed tolerance in most situations as a sunflower would be forced to shed the seeds in neglect, from once a week, to once a month. The young men were taught that laughter was more pleasurable than women and apologies for youthfulness.

Weakness and cowardly behavior was the last impressions that Abram would have liked to portray. His build was large, and his stance was larger, and any unscrupulous sensational recklessness was considered being 'yellow'. Whereas with Abram the cheap metaphors were ruled out and replaced by odds with Yarborough.

XXXI: Nutrition
YELLOW

Abram's apartment in Egypt was painted a light shade of butter vanilla. This was to reflect the sun's heat back into the atmosphere. His terrace, which was seventy feet above sea-level, was painted with the same colour as limestone, all into keeping the building as cool as possible. The only entrance to the terrace was from indoors unless someone was to parachute onto the deck. One late afternoon there came a rattle of taps from the terrace glass window. Abram walked to see two tall silhouettes appearing through his cream drapes to the terrace, he paused for a second and slid open the patio deck doors.

"Dee, Tamana, come in! You could have used the front doorbell, I had the door open. What are there any faults in your device?" said Abram after giving them a hug.

"Well we were just over there! Abram," said Derrick pointing at a yacht floating in the Mediterranean Sea. "Tammy thought she'd like to scare you by knocking on the window."

"Seriously Tam, the time-machine is not a toy," replied Abram.

"Who is it?" cried a voice from behind him.

"You've got yourself a mistress haven't you?" asked Tamana.

"Soon to be Mrs. Shiraz, so nice, nice," said Abram.

"Indigo?" asked Derrick.

"How did you know?" replied Abram.

"Ha. As you have no English rhyme and she had plenty," Derrick answered.

The warmth of the day began to cool as so did the wine placed on ice. Abram closed the doors facing north, and closed the drapes of the windows. The friends sat together to eat around a round table. They span laughter as a yo-yo on a string, drinking, singing, eating, laughing and spinning laughter still.

"My job; my job is to prevent infections across these climates, as well as bring drinkable water to all of the Sahara states from Sudan to Senegal. Mosquitoes transmit various diseases one being Yellow Fever, which is a fatal disease leading to vomits and hemorrhages. Now our Yggdrasil water pipe development across Africa will prove beneficial to all life. Some scorpions in the desert may not like it at first but I'm sure we can overcome that," said Abram as he made himself a banana shake. "I'll show you how we are planning to excavate the task, keep this smoothie on shake, I'll be back in a second."

Passing the ladies in the lounge whilst they giggled about what girls' giggle about, Abram ran into his study to bring back a scroll to show Derrick. He unrolled a map of Africa.

"This is the Red Sea; below this is the Gulf of Aden, leading to the Arabian Sea, leading to the Indian Ocean. This point we are to build a dam. Yemen has agreed for our company to mine there. So between Yemen and Djibouti, a dam will be made emptying the Red Sea from the rest of the waters. Now scattering from Egypt, Sudan, and Eritrea a network of pipes will cross east Sahara to the west, emptying out as oases throughout the desert. The pipe network would cross Sudan, Chad, Libya, southern Algeria, Niger, Mali and spill out from high altitudes of Mauritania, Guinea, Senegal, and Nigeria into the Atlantic Ocean," explained Abram. "Finally I don't want to know how this works out. We have spent years planning this, so if you have a Yellow Pages advertisement on Shiraz Industries, I don't want to know. Now have some smoothie and tell me what you think?"

126

XXXII: Nutrition
YELLOW

Youth can overcome all physical necessities thrown at them when they have mastered containing themselves. Yoga was practiced by Abram, but not as anyone could have imagined. The idea came by watching Jackie Chan and Jet Li fighting. Just the mare fact on tolerating the blocking pain made him think.

Self defense for army and against enemy, produce attacks only if ice is available readily. Firstly tense the hands against each other beginning in motion of pray. The muscles of thenar eminence are at the base of the thumb, moving the whole thumb moves the thenar eminence. Touching both hands together with palms open indicates the area of the hypothernar eminence. Folding the thumb over the palm to closely touch the pinky finger moves both eminences in action.

Tap right hypothenar eminence to left palm; rotate tapping of right hand with thenar eminence folded towards the palm. This will show four fingers, and tap gently rotate the wrist and massage eminences with the other hand. The rotation will allow for the left palm to slap the back of the right hand. Rotating right wrist carry to tap left palm, and approaching exertion change hands.

Hands are held together by finger-tips to help blood circulation, this in turn helps breathing, and this in turn helps a person remain sane. A man with one hand will close first and next finger with thumb to allow blood circulation. A man with no hands will have to press up against something, and hold onto Yahweh. Circulation maintained from the left hand works at a greater rate than closing the right.

From the left leg using a mixture of eminences strike the gastrocnemius medial and lateral head muscle. Work around this muscle to the shin back around. Striking, stretching, grapping, massaging down to the calcaneus, and around to massage the foot, with hard heavy blows as chopping actions with both hands. Breathe a little, stretch a little, and try not to yell. Fill the joy, move to the gigantic quadricep and hamstring. Balance right gluteus maximus at the edge of the bench, and work fully on left quadricep and hamstring. Shift all weight over to the left gluteus maximus, and start again from right gastrocnemius. Pulling, and stretching, and striking the muscles to expand the peptide bonds between the amino-acids, within the microfibrils, and overall expanding the muscle fibers.

Load weight onto lower body weight machine, and exert operation fully to maximize loading option with resistance. One brick, ten bricks, twenty bricks, thirty bricks, fifty bricks, seventy bricks, ninety bricks, ninety-one bricks, one-hundred bricks. Place feet back to gravity and rest. Lift again and rest. Lift again, rest and eat, to return again with eminences to pull the muscle fibers. Largest muscles in the body need to be stretched properly to be able to hold the required amounts of water as necessary.

Yet as martial arts are performed with best attentions the forces exerted from minimal effort can be quite harmful. Practice striking forearms with eminences, rotating whole arm to acquire maximal coverage. Tapping around bones to allow adaptation for more muscle tissue to expand over them, pulling, stretching, and covering all surfaces of pain to be covered by elastin and collagen.

Moving finally to involve the triceps, trapeziums and the pectoral majors. Striking with the eminences, striking a muscle group at a time, striking to withstand pain, and striking until there is no more wind left to expire. Time to sit up and inhale. Time to load with weight when stretching is over. Thud, thud, thud, slowly at first until all is done. Time to eat and to fill the muscles and bone, now the flesh, bones, cells and plasma are closer to the ground.

Careful consideration should be taken when performing this yoga. Studies of Abram's interest evolved him to investigate that this yoga was practiced to the tee for war. Abram reading this interest had read there was a Veda-yoga which was stopped from the Bhagavad-Gita, but some saw pass this caution and embraced an art of Kung-Fu through Siddhartha Gautama, and known as Sankar Yoga.

XXXIII: Nutrition
YELLOW

After coming home from his regular exercise routine, Abram yodeled to find out if his sons were back from school.

"Anyone home?!" he yodeled.

Slowly sounds started bouncing from the children's room as the door to their den opened. His sons came running towards him and began climbing him. He placed the youngest, Isaiah, who was three years onto the kitchen top, and Lester, at five years old on the kitchen stool.

"This is the diet of champions," Abram said.

He pulled the boys attention by blinking several times and twitching his toes. This helped them filter their excitement from seeing their father and concentrate on what was happening at present. Abram opened the fridge freezer and picked out three tubs of banana frozen-yogurt.

"Yogurt 'milk fermented' helps the bowel work well, plus tastes good. Packed full of vitamins and minerals that help us grow. You guys should drink a cup of milk a day, and have low-yogurt as lassi, and some water too. Your strength will be my own," said Abram. "What else helps with the movement of the bowel is cereal as oats, grains and barley. This makes the life's cellular physiology move, and that's what helps us shit."

"Dad said poo," said his youngest Isaiah.

"But dad only says poo," underlined Lester.

"Now try not to consume too much soda and fizzy stuff as you'll get gas and fart. Stick with water and lemonade that will hydrate you, and make you that much leaner. Now talking about getting larger, potatoes do the trick, small amount of unsaturated fats to limit cardiac problems. Eat a little salt from salty chips, as these help our synapses fire action potentials without hiccups. Moderately eat a little fat, but concentrate upon consuming complex carbohydrates as pasta and baked potatoes to hold down reserves of water. Beans and meat will provide amino acids to build more protein; in turn will make it easier for living. Thus to become big and strong as your old man, you'll have to follow these guidelines, and have one egg at least in the morning."

The egg, with or without yolk, but some agree how incredible that, that eggs' exist. What came first? An organic cell, which later developed to need a host, and later still developed to produce a delicious recipe of lipids needed to keep our bodies lubricated. One egg can be better than another, and the best omelet ever? Three eggs.

XXXIV: Nutrition
YELLOW

Tucking his younglings to sleep, Abram explained how the yum-yum in yams' was involved in digestion. His children yearned for his attention and learned from his teachings.

"Food is eaten to provide energy for us to stay alive and to think well. There are four main groups for food; carbohydrates, proteins, fats and fiber. Now you can remember what foods each of these components come from right?" he asked his two sons, as they made themselves comfortable before sleep.

They nodded, neither caring much at the age of three and five, so they stayed quiet to hear their father speak.

"Food also helps build Y-shaped antibodies that fight infections, and strengthens our immune systems. This way if we happen to fall over and hurt ourselves, the immune system will heal us up as good as new. This can come by if we eat well, and drink milk and water. Milk will help our bones and teeth to grow strong due to the calcium, and water to be drank frequently to keep us hydrated. If you feel a little woozy, then this is most probably because you are dehydrated, so get a glass of water or a sports drink to quench the thirst. This will keep your brain clogs ticking," said Abram. "Now who knows what the energy carrier is in the body?"

"ATP," they both said. "Adenosine triphosphate, to be in full," said Lester.

"Excellent! Well through food being digested, 'broken down' in the stomach, the carbohydrates enter aerobic respiration, 'living with oxygen' in organelles called mitochondria, in the cells of the body. Carbohydrates are broken down to glucose molecules and other sugars, and then these broken further to produce carbon dioxide; which we breathe out, and water; which is absorbed into cells, and ATP. This ATP is stored in muscle cells that when needed help move our muscles," Abram paused.

"What about protein, fats and fiber dad?" asked Lester.

"They all act for fuel for the body as they can produce ATP. However they have further individual importance as well. Aren't you guys tired already?" he asked them.

They looked at him and then each other with their puzzled look.

"Seems like you won't let me sleep until I finish this, I'll carry on until you two start yawning," said Abram and began taking a fake yawn.

134

"Stop that dad," said Lester.

"Well, proteins are consumed and after digested to provide nitrogen mostly to the body. This will help build muscles, and nucleic acids that are essential to replicate each cell's DNA, so we can live and heal. Some people's nucleic makeup gets mixed around and complications arise."

"Ha, ha, dad said makeup," said Isaiah.

Abram smiled: "Fat digested will help insulation in the bodies, keeping us warm in colds, and helping with structuring our cell membranes, plus fat provides faster releases of ATP when needed. However eating too much fatty-food as fried stuff with more oil will begin to weaken cell membranes and cause atherosclerosis to severe heart problems. Fatty foods are lovely to eat as their oil yields plenty of pleasure, that's why you feel great after eating fried chicken. Plus it tastes good. If you see someone with yellow skin, then that maybe due to their fat stores not breaking down fast enough, this is due to bile salts not being released from the gall bladder. They are known to have jaundice."

Abram watched his children's eyelids wither: "Now for fiber, fiber helps the passage of stools, which is why you see grandpa and grandma eating fiber, so they don't get too much constipation. Fiber, like sweet corn is not easily digested by the body and pass straight through into

135

our poo," Abram paused for remark. "The affectivity of digestion depends on the body's metabolism, which is inversely dependent on?"

"Dad said makeup," Isaiah said and began yawning.

Lester began yawning.

"The answer is, stress level," Abram finished and gave a larger yawn.

They all yawned again and went to yonder.

XXXV: Nutrition
YELLOW

The word for blood without any cells is called plasma, the plasma is yellow. The hemoglobin protein in the cells of blood contains iron. This iron is needed to carry oxygen. This oxygen is used to prevent anyone being anemic. The iron is important for maintaining an athlete's performance on regards for oxygen transportation and energy production. And without the iron the blood remains yellow.

Sleeping in bed with Susan dressed over in a yellow sari as he liked on Kajol, they both played whispers of intelligence until she mentioned another infant.

"Best thing to give a mother whilst growing a fetus would be protein and folate for synthesis of DNA, carbohydrates for energy, and of course iron," Abram had said.

"For the chance for us to have another baby, I'll feed her so she can be provided with antibodies to protect her from her father's digestive habits," said Susan.

"Oh and improving her on development of her jaw and teeth. I don't like the sound of that.

Sure it's lovely for the child's growth but I think we should wait a while. Only advantage I see is for you to return back to pre-pregnancy weight," replied Abram.

"You were meant to say 'Oh and reducing the chance of pre-menopausal breast cancer.'"

"Ha, ha, you said breast."

"You silly, now give me a daughter," insisted Sarah pushing herself onto Abram.

"You are as bad as the boys. No snacking in excess amounts. You'll grow resistant to fruits and vegetables, and more depended on chocolate and potato chips. Only one snack a day with three decent size meals. Learn to live your own life instead of consuming mine," resisted Abram.

"Hey I'm still young. No intestinal tract problems of constipation, if so I'll eat fiber. My liver is working fine thanks, thus keeping this body in shape. And my basal metabolism is ticking for you. Plus if my senses become reduced then I'll eat folate foods, vitamin B_6 and B_{12}, and a bowl of cereal more often. Hey honey can you smell my perfume? It's from Y'lang-Y'lang trees," she said slowly.

"Ok time to really slow down Susan, my head is pulsing," said Abram.

"I'll slow down if you give me what I want," Susan replied.

Abram thought long and hard for his actions and delivered to reward Susan with what she desired. He stretched to grab his stance on the cold marble floor and walked to the bathroom.

Later that night noise started being yelped from outside their home. The noises came across as yelling. They became more distinguishable and woke Abram and Susan from their sleep. The yelling was coming from their neighbours. The couple looked at each other. Abram grabbed his robe and Susan went to see if the children were awake. Abram opened the door to their home and walked out of his driveway towards the cries. Running out came two souls and three gunshots. His neighbour with a few shreds of clothes dropped to the floor, one gunshot had grazed Yama, and the third struck Abram's temple.

XXXVI: Future
BLACK

Traveling from three different locations the friends arrived to sound the bell to the side entrance of the theatre. The time of day was approaching dusk, and the time of year was chilled enough to see exhaled air condense into vaporized water clouds. Tyler bounced on the spot as he waited for Abram who was approaching from the distance. Tamana walked around the corner to see Tyler blowing clouds of warm air into the cold to see them evaporate. Abram increased his pace as he felt a shiver down his spine.

The door buzzed before Tamana could pull out her key, and Abram pushed his way in taking full opportunity towards quickly getting out of the cold. Abram was naturally from Africa, regardless that he had been born in Moscow, and being also as a baby elephant he preferred the warmth. He walked ahead of the other two into the basement of the theatre. Derrick was on his favorite couch throwing playing cards over a ludo board game.

"The roll of the dice can be fixed. Shall we witness our pray being answered?" suggested Derrick. "I owe a favor for a lost soul, which without my practice would have only fallen into theory. And this favor I have to pay in person. Do you remember the break in on the night I first tested my invention Abram?"

"Yes, Derrick," Abram replied.

"Time to place equities in motion. I know you guys must have been anticipating this moment; well the moment has finally arrived. The sense of déjà vu in the back of your minds will be lifted," said Derrick. "As Peter I, changed the capital of Russia to St. Petersburg in 1713, I can guarantee that Moscow, first founded by Prince Yuri Dolgoruky in 1147, will always be the capital of Soviet Russia."

"Wasn't Moscow always the capital?" asked Tamana.

"Before Peter I, the capital of Russia was Moscow, however this changed and later changed back in 1918 March 12th, my birthday, due to Moscow leading the countries finance and transportation of goods," replied Abram.

"By 'goods' he means everything that Russia has to offer; coal, oil, metals, gas, military hardware. All the smart people of Russia began to live in Moscow, and constructions of electric power generators, nuclear power, rail transportations, building materials and medical expertise concentrated themselves here," added

Tyler. "However I have no idea what Derrick is getting on at? I rather not ask him."

Tamana and Abram chuckled slightly as they understood Tyler.

"If you guys haven't eaten I suggest we eat before we leave. The trip will make you feel a little woozy and I need you Abram, Tyler, to be on guard. Can't afford to make any mistakes," carried on Derrick.

"Have you been drinking?" asked Tamana as she walked over to him.

He kissed her as she leaned in. He held her by the waist and sat her down beside him.

"If all goes well then when we return we will still have television transmission, the Moscow Metro, and the XXII Olympic Games in 1980. Just to prepare you that if all turns soar then the deaths of millions from Iosif Stalin reign in Russia to keep communism, would be better for the world than this experiment," said Derrick. "Nothing to worry about, as I said I owe a favor in time, not like I am trying to take over Japan as well."

Derrick sat back and looked up at the ceiling. He exhaled a long thin gust of air from his lungs; he inhaled fresh air and looked over at the ludo board. He began to explain the travel to his friends. Abram and Tyler found the words coming from Derrick hard to imagine but they felt strength from his expressions that they played along.

"So let me get this right. After we show the others the importance of the task you will take us to see how Siberia becomes industrialized?" asked Tyler.

"But before that to Quebec City? Why is that?" mentioned Abram.

"The strength in our worship and the belief in faith will allow us to do just that," replied Derrick. "I want good things to happen for our Lord. Jesus was strong on his decision to be struck with iron just as I am certain nothing will go wrong. Now let us stand and brace one another together in pray."

After they sat in silence for several minutes, Derrick showed them the invention he had made. The staff like looking rod brought uncertainty to Derrick's friends. He asked them all to hold and feel the contraption. He explained how the dials worked and asked his friends to repeat what they had just heard from him. Then Derrick stood and stamped the ground gently with the time-machine. The T.M. extended in length. He propped up against it and spent a time to pray beside it. Derrick nudged his friends closer to him and pressed a button. Whilst holding Abram and the machine, Abram held Tyler who held Tamana who held Derrick and all realized that they no longer could move or blink. And as fast as a lightning charge they vanished out of sight.

143

XXXVII: Future
BLACK

Thousands of footsteps, some to see, some to experience, some to feel like progress was being made in the twenty-first century, and some to have coffee travelled south on Zamoskvoretskaya Metro to Domodedovskaya Station. And then to relax amongst thousand others as they traveled to and from Domodedovo Moscow International Airport.

"I didn't mean any harm. I was looking for money or food. There was no intention in my blood to cause any harm to anyone inside when I tried to break in. I was raised in the old Soviet. My great-grandfather fought in 1905's Russian Revolution for the working people, and my grandfather survived until my father was born, and my father died in World War II, so I was raised with my mother, until she gave me up to my father's sister and fled to God knows where. Since then I have been moving from foster home to foster home until I found the Salvation Army, who moved me to where Tyler found me," said Craig.

"Who knows if you would have caused harm? You may have panicked and hurt someone or caused psychological pain," replied Tyler.

"There is no possible way to see what disturbance you may have caused and I made sure of that," concluded Derrick. "From the 11 million people in Moscow I'm sure you would have hurt someone from your desperation. But don't worry about that now."

"Why not consider working for missionary groups, giving hope to the less fortunate. The way I see it, you have shelter and you have food. May not be a palace but better than living in a hospital," added Tamana.

"What can missionary work do for me?" asked Craig.

They all looked at each other and smiled then looked back at Craig.

"Craig, mission work is not about you. Think about this; a U.S. Ambassador recites in Moscow who manages St. Petersburg, Vladivostok and Yekaterinburg for the American people who visit Moscow, or if Abram wishes to visit the States," said Derrick.

"I have no intention of moving, I like Moscow," said Abram.

"There is also a Diplomatic Represenger for Russia in the U.S. for Russians living there. He works as a missionary for Houston, New York, San

Francisco and Seattle from their capital. So you can help Russians with your history for any Russian Embassy over the world," said Derrick to warm Craig's love for his fathers.

"Wow, for the information you know you should become mayor of this city," said Craig.

"I would rather be the President of the U.N. however I don't see that happening."

"Ha, that's funny. See that happening," said Abram.

Derrick smiled towards Abram and said: "Russia, the white, blue and red, last year 2008, cost $1.75 trillion to buy, represented by the official exchange rate. I'll either have to be Bill Gates or make the country bankrupt. The U.N. would be more practical."

"Ha, more practical," said Tamana.

They all looked over at her: "What? I just wanted to join in," she nodded through to Abram and he nodded back at her.

Derrick nodded at Abram and Tamana then said, "Delicious."

"Ha, delicious," they replied and laughed a little as Derrick smiled back.

After a few seconds; "To make the country bankrupt I'd…" continued Derrick.

Derrick paused for a second, stretched over the table and picked up a roll of bread. Looking at them and second glancing Craig he said: "Initially we have to make the place worthless and workless, no people, no animals, no beef, no milk, no grains, no sunflower seeds, no fruit, nor veg and no life to grow or trade to bury." Derrick stared at the table as the sentence caught up to his friends.

"Best for you to stick to videogames Dee," said Tyler faking to clean his tear sockets.

Derrick threw half the roll of bread onto the floor. Later he would dispose of it, but as for then he kept gaze on his friends instead of the piece of bread on the floor.

"My caruncula lacrimalis itches, do I have something in my eye?" asked Tamana staring at the bread on the floor. "I can hear a pair of nines they are tapping every so softly."

"Missionary work then huh? Where can I start something like that?" asked Craig.

"You could help with the mosques," suggested Tyler. "We have over two million Muslims here in Moscow with only four mosques. I hear they are planning to make another two; you can help arrange classroom tables and chairs if you like. Come with me to the next pray, I'll introduce you to some people. That's one way to bite the bullet."

"Sounds like a start Craig. You can start by carrying my old books to them. Most have fun stuff like math but I do have comics, and books on history and invention," said Derrick.

147

"I have writings by 1799 poet, A.S. Pushkin," said Craig.

"Yes that's a start. Like Muhammad Ozbeg, approving Ivan Kalita, the Prince of Moscow in the early 14th century to collect taxes from all of Russia. You will be given assistance in collecting people to help with Allah's work," added Tyler. "Now that doesn't sound so bad right?"

"Plus you are not that bad to look at either," added Tamana. "I mean you are easy on the eyes and people like that."

They all looked over at her; Derrick leaned over to whisper something in her ear.

"Do you think I can be the knight on the white horse slaying the dragon, like the knight on the Moscow flag?" asked Craig.

"Sure you can Craig," replied Tamana.

"Plus that knight still has to be discovered. They made him in '95, before we started college, along with the anthem and emblem of Moscow that his identity still remains fiction," added in Abram. "You can be that knight even though I wanted to be him first."

"You both can be knights," added Tamana.

"There's only one knight on the flag. And I don't know how to ride a horse. What if Abram knows how to ride the horse and is a better knight? What should I do then?" asked Craig.

"I think you should move to St. Petersburg and work in Baltika," said Abram.

"Well if I was a beer, I would be a Baltika."

"If I was a beer, I'd be a Fosters."

"If I was a wine, I'd be a white one," continued Tamana.

"If I was a white woman, I'd be Kate Middleton, hands down," added Tyler.

"If I was a white man, I'd be Ryan Rayolds," returned Derrick.

"If I was a black man, then I'd be Denzel Washington. No, no, yes, Denzel," Craig said.

"If I was a monument I'd be the Washington Monument. I don't know why I said that," laughed a little Tyler. "I'd be the Holy Kaa'ba."

"If I was a monument or landmark, I'd be Madison Square Garden on game night!"

"Nice, nice," returned Tamana. "If I was constellation of stars, I'd be Orion's Belt."

"Nice," complimented Abram. "If I was a Hindu god, I'd be Shiva."

"Thought you'd be Krishna," said Tamana.

"You are Krishna," replied Abram.

Derrick looked over, "Well if I was a super hero, I'd be Superman. And if I was a super villain I'd be Megatron! Leader of the Decepticons."

"Jesus Christ, have mercy," Craig added.

"If I was a vegetable, I'd be a potato. And if I was a fruit, I'd be a watermelon, as you like that!"

149

XXXVIII: Future
BLACK

L anding to affiliate the future of Moscow, Derrick placed north and east latitude coordinates from Greenwich median to his time-machine to stand square on one roof of Stalin's buildings. Prime choice was chosen due to importance of still being in existence. The M.S.U. building had survived since 1755, and reconstructions through three centuries allowed Derrick to believe that the building would still be intact for a further three centuries.

Pulling into the circumferential tangent from the center of the sun to the change in the earth's orbital position, the time he wanted to land in was June 12th 2309. This was to be a Russian National Holiday celebrated since 1994, and resulted from a constitution enabling Russia to be presented with a universal life. The children would dance to celebrate this holiday away from communism and into a diplomatic Russia. Derrick would analyze on his travel if Russia Day was still being celebrated, this would enable him to calculate that earth had become a diplomatic planet.

As he landed from space he instantly felt his lungs expand. The usual fog of Moscow's atmosphere had been diminished remarkably. Derrick felt uneasy within the same habitat. He inhaled and looked across the horizon clockwise from standing facing south. The sky was noticeably clear regardless that this time of year was brought into hot summers, however something was greatly changed. Stepping to the side of the building Derrick looked over to the street below. People were celebrating within the street, evidently Russia Day still existed.

Everything that Derrick remembered about the economy of Moscow seemed to have been enhanced. The divergence from where Derrick had previously seen had changed by a reduction in pollution. This once heavily industrialized city seemed to have less smog. Air pollution had seemed to have reduced and the distinction that he had felt was a change in smell. The city not only smelled cleaner but the air was thinner and easier to breathe. The prospect of less air pollution would have resulted to improve agriculture and less soil impurity. The result from using hydrogen and electrically fuelled vehicles within the cities had paid well to the environment.

Derrick adjusted the gyroscope on the staff and moved from the roof of the building to the ground below. Waiting for the fragments of ions that dissembled his space in time to move with the coordinates that he targeted on the street beside the building, the staff moved him through the stone of the building, and he was to stand firmly as time found him space on the busy street of Lomonosovskiy Prospekt.

He approached a newsstand picked up a newspaper and gave the man a few rubles. The man looked at him with a puzzled look like he was some foreigner from a distant planet. Derrick stood waiting for the man to say something. The man waited for Derrick to say something. They waited standing in the same pose as when Derrick reached out to hand the man money. The man began to laugh and carried on working. Local citizens walked pass the man's stand and collected drinks, food, newspapers, candy, anything but a packet of smokes and left without paying the man anything. Derrick stood waiting for someone to pay the man. 2309 was printed on the papers. Derrick asked the man why he was not collecting money.

"Nobody works for money son. Where are you from?" asked the man.

"What do you mean? What about food? What about tax?" asked Derrick.

"You are not from here traveler are you? We have stopped chopping trees long ago. Since beginning of the last century we live entirely to better ourselves. All necessities are shared accordingly and signed for when received. This enters the database which compares the number of members in a family and daily consumption. Now where are you from?"

"I've just been away for a while. What about luxuries? What about education? Is this for the entire world?"

"Yes it's you," said the news man with gesture not to push the man into interrogation. "Luxuries are not so necessary as long as people have families. They can always have what they need but excess of anything is counted for. I see you have been asleep for some time."

"How do people live?" said Derrick and looked at the man's heart.

"Man you have been asleep for a while. We are all given living quarters, some more extravagant than the others, but all equipped with unionism to work, live and enjoy life away from war. Some say life is meaningless now, but I can go on holiday whenever I like, wherever I like, and for how long I like. You have been in the space station for some time now haven't you?"

"Something like that. Thanks for the paper."

"Enjoy Russia Day," returned the newsman.

The previous acting impressions of life for Russia were remembered by toxic radioactive wastes that filtered into the globe. These were bound to be stopped. One of the smartest places in the world, and indisputably one of the strongest in terms of defeating 1941 Germans at the Battle of Moscow had changed the world's economy. Six hundred years from murders, drug trafficking, and slanderous distribution of weapons, Derrick could go back to where he was from and fall asleep. He stepped away from the newsstand with his time-machine disguised as a walking stick and walked into the shadows of the university. The wind stopped blowing around Derrick as he turned the time-machine on and returned back into the comfort his couch in 2010.

Russia had changed the face of the world. The one most heavily industrialized country besides America had approached an eco-friendly future. Being the lead in scientific development they had managed to stabilize the use of un-renewable natural resources (fossil fuels), and place renewable natural resources to work. Energy from hydroelectric power, wind turbines and hydrogen fueled pistons all emitting water as byproduct followed to bring a fresher appearance to universal days.

XXXIX: Evolution
ORANGE

Overwrought from curiosity on where man had come from, Derrick balanced his views to agree that consciousness was given to all animals. All animals' conscious was to their ownership of their own fate, which lived in harmony to their personal habitat. Any animal considered not upholding to their own consciousness was outcaste, and later eaten by the earth to allow the growth of more organisms.

Man had evolved on dependency of any other animal, either by a unique cell or growth of mutation. Initially their consciousness fell into providing for their families and communities. Later conflicts from opposite ends of Orange River, led to man declaring power to protect their communities from those that were more suited to survive. Not to misunderstand the consciousness of every beast that beauty resided in a manner to respect a superior being. As animals prowled to eat whilst others grazed, they all began to understand that another creature was still yet to overcome.

Animals felt overwhelmed when food was not scarce as because their cells were nourished away from starvation. Lions and lionesses would watch their cubs play as ordinarily as most animals' would become to please a superior being. Naturally there is only tendency to remain numb whilst life degrades everything, however why is there an overbalance to feel emotion? Derrick wished to find the root of this question.

Oxygen was a necessity for all land, sea and sky animals. From plants using gases as carbon dioxide to release oxygen as a byproduct, filling some of the atmosphere, this led to the creation of other organisms that brought balance to the equation with nitrogen, filling most of our atmosphere. Sea organelles laid eggs on shores just as the mitochondrial eukaryotic cell established themselves from prokaryotic chloroplasts, leading to marine meiosis.

Animals evolved before 4 million years ago, and from 1.5 million years ago the dark coloured African Ape, began to form a branch of dark coloured hominins. One meter tall the species developed branches of its own likeness from Australopithecus to Homo habilis, to Homo floresiensis and Homo sapiens. The ossification developed the brain in the man-like people to become larger. Anthropologists studied skulls from the size of a grapefruit to average man capacity. The branch of Homo sapiens ovulated more following a better survival factor.

Far from observation the African Apes presented themselves to survive with an opportunistic gene pool of hominins to the land of India. (This observation reaches times of mythology before that of science). Hominins that evolved in the nourished land of India over 1.5 million years ago travelled over the Himalayan Alps and overlapped sand dunes for the curiosity of exploration, where the survival of the fittest strengthened them into more cultured humans.

In October 2004, in the Indonesian Islands of Flores, anthropologists found a cache of bones resembling a hominid of Homo floresiensis. In isolation the specie had not evolved since the departure from Africa, 94,000 years ago. The specie became extinct 12,000 years ago, whereas from 150,000 years ago, the common Homo sapiens dominated. Finding a remote cave of hominids the scientist analyzed wrist bone appendages to discover another branch of the Homo family. They were from the African Ape branch, such as from orangutans.

Once evolution occurred, some family members survived. Overall man came from ape differing in sizes to best suit their habitat. Plus their curiosity to survive gained them skills to hunt, craftsmanship to building tools and spears, which they passed to their families, and to the more opportunistic Homo sapiens sapiens.

XL: Evolution
ORANGE

According to opportunistic science the land would overflow by water. The infrared radiation of the sun's rays would penetrate the earth's atmosphere easily as the ozone layer would tear more. This would increase the temperature of the waters to melt the polar icecaps. Mostly everything will become flooded either by rain or raise in sea level. There's no reason to expect this happening in the close future. On the contrary draught could expand leading to fewer crops for the expanding populations on Earth.

Within some deserts of the world as for Chile, Africa and Australia, animals were adapted to survive. After all moisture had been pulled away from the ground by air currents or cactuses, animals had to reserve water for the drought seasons. Man, Nelson Mandela, M. Carey, and the rest of the humans, had moved far from these habitants as their biological suits were not made to survive hot days and cold nights. The desert over the earth's equator would increase by $5^{\circ C}$ every hour, along with sandstorms built to roast hives from the pulsating heat would make it unbearable to survive.

Enormous animals are usually herbivores like elephants, kangaroos and camels known to eat hay, roots of plants, rice balls and oranges. Carnivores like tigers, lions, birds of prey, some spiders and reptiles, like rattlesnakes become adapted to hot climates, but when food is scarce they resort to death in the shade. Lizards of the desert take cover under rocks, and like some animals come out only at night to stretch their legs or find food as other animals. Omnivores eat like herbivores and carnivores; they possible can eat them as well. If not they eat eggs for saturates pardoning that they are unfertilized.

Tropical climates allow for thousands of animals to ovulate and breed. The source of life between rainforests and dry suburban regions vary in constitution of animals. Nevertheless there is still evidence of life in the quietest regions of this globe. All adapted to fit their main goal, to feed and breed.

Moreover the orange sun doesn't provide any form of life on other planets of the solar system except this one. Regardless all species believe in their own heaven or to become human. Only under specific conditions did life start and evolve on this planet. Let us pray that there is another one.

XLI: Evolution
ORANGE

The Catholic Church was neglected by some Christian followers whom orientated Christian Orthodox sublimity to the book of Genesis. This orthodox practiced evidence and just causes to the followings of Christ. To overestimate the Father's passage on creating life on earth through six eras, (overseen with the Father) Derrick believed that animals either wished to be man or with man.

As the Lord would require all life to enter His realm, all life was to be judged accordingly before He could make this happen. The only matter of confusion arose when animals exceeded the rate of acceptance, thus the Lord lost the right to judge everyman fairly. Once man had learnt to make fire, they were given sighting of God. Saying; man was allowed to have children as early as possible just in case one had to be placed down. Sightings as such made the whole process that much swifter to the earth's orbit around the seasons.

On a thunderous day lightening crackled across the skies of Africa, and before rain began to pour a tree was struck with a lightning bolt. Flames of fire spread throughout the tree's branches and crisped the leaves to ashes. Every animal in the vicinity fled in freight except for one man who witnessed the tree burning. A branch of fire disembarked to the ground and the man took this torch to heat his home. Others later followed to find out the root of fire.

The spark for fire can be made possible by burning tinder, leaves, grass, bark and resin. Later kindling as small twigs and sticks were added on sparked tinder to grow the fire, later still firewood found from dead trees can be added to grow the fire further. The ignition was sparked by smacking stones together to fly a spark to the tinder.

So animals not only gained consciousness from Pangaea, but intelligence as they moved from origin Africa to the north to become Caucasian, cracking of the continental plates to become Red-Indian, through the mid-east to become Persians, climbing against forced winds of the Himalayas to become Oriental, over generations.

The offspring initially had difficulty on maintaining their curiosity on why other animals were allowed to play whereas they were forced to work. Overlooking the sand dunes of civilizations that were made in the time of the Pharos, no child overnight was given pride of his ownership with the land. Impossible to agree with ostentation for those that do than those that do not was better. The oxidization of the sand from rust was gleefully appreciated by civilizations, which then built their own kingdoms to orchestrate freedom, and then to divide and conquer.

An oxymoron description to help those children with wealth, as also the children without ostentation, was decided by one. What was the objective for the humble to help the crude through opsonin? When the crude operated obstructive barriers ahead of them, Marshall Mathers sang to reach the osmotic offspring of the new generation that there was three ways to live: to build credit, to learn to build credit, or to learn and build credit.

Oratory conduct should be spoken by an orator. Their words should be filled for acceptance that neither the superior beings' should be close to hunger or famine. Nevertheless the next evolution was psychological and regarded to be on approach to Nirvana. The new evolved man was away from predator Ospreys and towards wisdom as Great Horned Owls. Just for instance the Lord gave to some with owlish behavior the fire-ant off chance that there was still something left to owe.

XLII: Religion
BLACK

Craig Goncharov opened the main entrance to the New Opera Theatre to let in Derrick from his arrival back home. There was pace in his stride as he brushed past Craig heaving his bags not to hurt him. Derrick walked past the lobby of the theatre straight to stage one, ground floor. Tyler was sitting in the main row listening to Abram standing beside the stage front. The curtain was closed to reflect dark burgundy. Derrick dropped his bags close to the aisle and stepped onto stage.

"I need you to explain a few things to me Tyler," insisted Derrick. "When I arrived to Toronto, crossing over to the States, I was stopped by a U.S. Customs Officer. This officer looked at me as I was shit, and I think it was because I was wearing that warm scarf you had gave me. Now instead of him directly facing me and swearing, he began swearing under his breath towards the computer. He didn't know how to listen! Mmmmm. Now I know girls can just speak shit on the off chance and at random moments, ruin whole football games, this is all to acquire attention, or just because they didn't know how to tell a joke. I know it can be distracting, I hate them for it, but you're at work, no need to involve me!"

"Steady man, slow down. Did you look at her feet to let her know she was at work?" interrupted Tyler.

Derrick continued: "Well the place was filled with all people of all ages and of children, some learning how to speak, others learning how to live, and more finding the reason on why to like the customs officer. This 'man' with his counterpart, two 'men' now, swearing amongst themselves behind their petty desk and chewing gum whilst being on the job. Don't they have a lack of jobs in the States? What a shit way to enter a country that lives within by the Lord's words. Now these two are grinning and smirking amongst themselves, chewing gum and stealing moments to provoke me to swear, so they can take me behind closed doors..."

"Have you eaten?" asked Tamana.

"Not now Tama, I won't be able to enjoy it. I just feel like using my work to destroy that officer, and his family, making sure I meet no one like that anymore. Dick-head! There am I raising funds so his children have a steady life, and there's him abusing the Lord's will. What a pair of morons! They're paid much more than half the people I know, and they abuse the right to be civil," continued Derrick. "Ha ha ha ha, they can't listen to music," and he began to Om in his mind.

"I'm sorry to hear that Derrick. So what do you want me to explain?" asked Tyler.

"Teach me how to relax. I really feel like I should make a list of individuals I would like to send to hell now ..."

"There's *fajr;* the dawn pray, which is a compulsory pray, there's *dhuhr;* the noon pray, and there's *ishaa;* the night pray, there's also *tahajjud;* a voluntary pray at anytime of the day. Now with these we seek *istighfaar;* the forgiveness from Allah for our thoughts. Come with me to *ishaa* tonight, once you showered and eaten," insisted Tyler. "Best you come tonight and then for *fajr* in the morning, I want you to find *makrooh* after what you just said."

"What's that?" asked Derrick whilst he paced to-and-fro across his theatre's stage.

"Due to *sharee'ah*, the code of law written in the Holy Qur'an, we are to walk away from discouraging acts, and with *makrooh* we will be rewarded from abstaining against the *haraam* of *sharee'ah,* and this is *fatwaa*, the religious verdict."

"I like the sound of that. I praise our Father for you Tyler; you have relaxed me greatly by *makrooh.* Blessed be He who is able to do all things."

165

"*Rahimahullah,* may Allah place his mercy on him, and we wish *radi Allahu'anhum,* that Allah be pleased with them. Note how your thought process is gathering the negatives Derrick, I need you to stay calm man, otherwise I will help you to conquer God's final verdict. Now don't force that on me, I rather have *sunnah,* but for you the Qur'an is in favor, so don't argue with the people of scripture. The Jews and Christians will be judged just like the rest of us."

"You should allow Prophet Muhammad, and Lord Jesus, and me, to work and love you as you have loved us Derrick," said Tamana.

"Yes, trust Tamana, and with the meaning of her name in scripture, trust us," forwarded Tyler.

"Breathe man, breathe strong and hard, blow all that bad air out of you, and inhale our air to fill your lungs. Breathe hard Derrick. I cleared my smoke filled lungs after you saved me, and I made sure that when I spoke to you I would exhale only clean air," said Craig, and exhaled with force to the ceiling above him, then inhaled gently to see Derrick slow his pace across the stage floor. "When I accepted Muhammad with my Christian faith I was filled with tears, thank you Tyler for being merciful yourself."

"*Saheeh,*" said Derrick looking at Tyler.

Tyler shook his head and said: "You don't have to pray as *rak'ah,* but do pray and pray for the well. Try not to be induced by the jealousy of other men, plus I'm scared of you Derrick as you have the power not only to change lives but to change all time as we know it."

"Doesn't the scripture read, 'Allah does not like evil except by the person that He has wronged?' Well He has wronged you Tyler; you didn't deserve your fate to be presented as it did. Thus I ask you, should I have mercy?" enquired Derrick and blinked at Tyler sitting down on the first row.

"I maintain *tasbeeh,* something that the Bible describes as, 'To glorify the Father and reject any imperfections attributed to Him,'" replied Tyler. "Believe in the Lord your God."

"And that is *fatwaa* too?" asked Derrick approaching him.

"Masha'allah," Tyler said, "Meaning as God has willed."

"*Saheeh*, that's right" replied Derrick. "*Shokra,* meaning, thank you," he continued. He began breathing normal and went to hug Tyler.

"I like living in the light with Allah, Allah's light, Light, but I would definitely be cautious of those two. I can see them clearly through your eyes," said Tyler as Derrick approached him.

Tyler shook his head and said: "Alternative to maintaining fingers and thumbs together you can go stand close to the wall, enough to keep arm's length. As like surgeons might during operations. Do what I do at times and prop against the wall with one finger, arm high above your head against a curtain rail, breathe and get back to some love," returned Tyler. "And when done look over the wall to the horizon."

XLIII: Religion
BLACK

Dust gathering on old cobwebs accumulated to greater masses at some corners of the main lobby in Dormition Cathedral. Outlined against the gray background of cold stone and tarred painted wood the spiders would nest. They would collect dust that had built during services which kept areas of human services clean.

All friends came to worship here and at times they would have come altogether. Standing and singing hymns from psalms and proverbs brought warmth to light their souls. Amongst the cool atmosphere laid between the tiled floor and the clayed roof the sound of admiration for Christ remained as sharp as the thorns were to His head.

So a miracle was performed when Jewish scholars read and taught. Moses picked up a snake, and later man came to deliver the snake back to the Lord. Another miracle was spoken through the Father as blind men, paralytic persons, the sick, and unwell were healed in an instant with the faith of the one as His alone freed all injustices. I'll stand with you awhile where you can always see me.

Witnesses came to believe that water tasted like wine, and compromising love allowed for some ladies to be forgiven through oil and lanterns. Furthermore Solomon's Kingdom was greater than all the sand on the seashores, and allowed safety from all backgrounds, may that be of cooks or princesses. Later the Romans bowed to allow righteousness to flow for all human-kind from building roads and aqueducts.

Through the closing doors behind the backs of the souls that entered the cathedral, love was closed within the building. The building represented the body of Christ, and after three days of reconstruction the wounds were allowed to heal for the gospels' to speak. The men spoke freely as they spoke with one name in mind, and that name came through the truth and grace of Jesus Christ. The law was given to Moses and witnessed by the friends, whilst the Father witnessed them from the neighbouring mountain.

The masoretes listed twelve prophets and later twelve apostles were grown for Jesus to find. Just as the friends would find dark red blood of the Christ fall bringing hallowed sand to Jerusalem, they sang in church for no more prophets for all time. And they prayed from Matthew and Luke, The Lord's Pray, all in one voice and one sound, to forgive Jesus Christ trespassing through man, which the Father had already declared as holy, and for the Son of God to forgive them, all in which to bring us to the Promised Land.

Gather your belongings, rise to your feet and leave. Words were cried with red fury eyes that to stop and stare at them for longer would leave that person never to be remembered. Great tears in the eyes of the Father, and the Father needed everyone, that those that used the devil would be ignoring the Lord's generosity.

As Saul began to realize the evil spirit of God dwelling within him, he called for David as the Lord's spirit was with him. That only David could release Saul from the evil spirit of God as the Lord's spirit was within him. The role that Father left on them could have only been forgiven by the Father, thus Saul finding himself closer to David, who played the harp and repented on many killed by him, that the Father forgave him also.

Nevertheless a judge's counterpart was not forgiven but thrown into the depths of hell. No moments to repent. Momentarily he should have left with a lantern instead of continuously striking his partner. The crime that her husband had performed enabled her to kill him quickly, but gave her great pain. Thus her decision for the rock that landed from the hands of the victim into the head of the defendant, allowed Deborah to be more than remembered.

Across the pages of scripture learnt amongst the friends, through the dull observed nights that were felt by them, only one felt true compassion through oppression. Like Paul wrote his findings as not to write them would have resulted into nothing. And Paul, a prisoner and chained to another prisoner in Philippians, wrote his memoirs in the cell's heat, in sweat and shit that would have resulted into nothing, leaving everything to be ignored and no world to have ever been discovered.

The apocalypse declared through the faith of Jesus Christ and the witnesses of John the apostle, resulted to more arriving to believe in the true will of the Father. What a story to make up about nothing and nonsense, that that story itself could be hocus pocus. Nevertheless the story made the rest of the Holy Bible seem that much more real. Especially that of Peter's fishes to be a fool of witchcraft from Jesus, that later condemned himself to phrase judgment starting with the family closest to God, declaring that Jesus Christ was the path to the light.

In Moscow, 1468, was born Basil, later renamed as St. Basil the Blessed (Fool for Christ). As in 1547, he saved the people from a rampaging forest fire that covered the entire town. His faith in Christ allowed him to prophesize the coming of the fire early. He died in 1552. During 1555 – 1560, St. Basil's Cathedral was built in Red Square to

172

commemorate him and give him a place to rest. Later in 1588, Tsar Fyodar Ivanovich, built the Ninth Chapel across from St. Basil's Cathedral to grave the Fool for Christ, and allow him to rest over the times of refurbishments to the cathedral. Finally declaration to the outstanding belief of Petr Baranovsky for Christ, that the architect in 1930 stood on the steps of St. Basil's Cathedral threatening Iosif Stalin, that he would slice his own neck if anything was to happen to the magnificent monument.

As for Judaism and Islam coinciding in most degrees of service to the Father; the strong foundation of rituals maintained the importance for them to worship and pass over that importance. People had to be hard hearted to allow custom for the Father to be appreciated. That in order to allow God's word to be maintained, that heaven is open, and the road for salvation is to help thy brother and thy sister and thy neighbour. They read and wrote to learn from the Father's word which kept them growing strong.

India seems to be further in the past than any other country. This nation had declared themselves to have heard the word from God initially. The One Spirit received from Indra, who was recorded in scripture through the Rig-Vedas books (5000 B.C), and later the Bhagavad-Gita (3000 B.C), teaching children the words from

173

Shree Krishna. Hinduism kept love in Father's name along with stick dances that kept demons out of earth. Unfortunately time played course and people naturally progressed to sinful acts of crime and sexual immorality. Somewhere along the line people bread more than they worshipped or worked. This led some scholars back into the forests and jungles to write about dealings with suffering in the Upanishads' scripture.

People divided from teachings of Hinduism to find refuge again in God's grace, which led to Islam growing exponentially in the golden era of the 7th century. From Arabian influence to those of Abbasid Caliphs, translations of Prophet Muhammad, his words spread throughout India to reduce the pace of injustice spreading, and beautiful monuments were made to compliment the love from the Father to mother Earth.

Islam presented strict rules in maintaining one's self from sin and towards the liking of the Father. Roughly at this time Abraham received the word of God and spread Judaism from the Middle East. Most likely due to preservation of land the Torah was neglected from India, due to the separation of the Islamic community and the blind eye developing in India. The Torah listed times of growth from first human civilization, i.e. much similarity to Sanskrit scripture by faith in the Spirit left by the heavens for a world not yet unraveled.

Not surprising that when all faiths had pride upon themselves, and with Hindustan broken into many kingdoms, the British penetrated in the nineteenth century. Eventually hypocrisy was lifted off the Christian Cross, and carried into the nation to mark the resting spot for Apostle Thomas.

The British left Hindustan in the mid-twentieth century to be separated into Pakistan and India, on the agreement that India would be a diplomatic nation. Islamic worshipped freely in their right and Hindus worshipped in their right. Overall they both began to worship for forgiveness and love for their neighbour.

The Chinese community found acceptance in Buddha, from India, to live peacefully amongst themselves. They prayed to things that had importance in the world, like animals, like weather, like music. Buddhism demonstrated personal reflection to their survival only in the Father's nature. Om Namah Shivaya, as Om as a long sound to be held for body and mind relief was carried further by Buddhist. Theoretically the separation of tongue would have led to disobedient language to be used. Hypocrisy against worship would not have been tolerated by the Spirit. Shiva's finding's was delivered to the Chinese by Siddhartha Gautama.

So the Father masqueraded as a Jew, and brought Lord Jesus Christ, to be presented for all man-kind to learn the word that all men were

175

looking for, and that was love. This however could have only been learnt until Christianity was born by His resurrection. Once Christianity, the new religion of the Common Era was born, and the word of Lord helped worshippers of all religions bring laughter, and the word of salvation to dying souls of the eastern and modern world.

And as for this from today and forever the simple nature of one man had brought balance to the whole world. If one was not spiritual then they would be an atheist. Distinguishing the two is a matter of asking the man which scripture he reads. Now whatever religion one may follow they too will come to realization that the cross is to be approached by all men who wish to enter heaven. Now to make things easier for the forth coming generations, allow them to live for the Father through the acceptance of the Messiah. That those that repent realize that there's no way back.

XLIV: Religion
BLACK

Born again into a new development of species with lines of scripture to be repeated only in this manner. Entirely a change in aberration from once what was illustrated by some false callers for Prophet Muhammad. Those false callers of intensively repeating callings of our Father were undeniably begging to be punished. Common callings erased from crying Father's name to praising His name instead was to be the final call allowed by us.

The Moscow Grand Mosque was refurbished with shades of light paint, which covered the outer walls and reflected a little more light to the surrounding buildings. Inside beside the basins, sinks, plumbing, cool tiled floors and shoe holds allowed flowers to decorate the area of pray. The flowers were replaced once they began to wither. Two more mosques were constructed outside the busy vicinity of the city. All mosques paid emphasis to strengthening the young amongst humbling themselves.

Is it so the elder Muslim men don't have problems with arthritis because of praying motion?

Whatever it may be a fraction of the population are finding this difficult to do, beats the whole purpose to finding their own answers. Praying should primarily be open to hands, hands together, crossed thumbs and then finger-tip to finger-tip and push. Calling this praying with Allah was strong, and could be done anywhere at any time with confidence. Rolling the fingers between each other by passing them through each other; playing with them when beads were not around made all of Lord's men have fun, whilst counting the seconds.

Children targeted for abuse, crime and suffering were replaced by children eating well, smiling graciously and humbling the hearts of elders. The smell had changed from burnt paint that presented itself for half a decade to the sweet smell of blooming flowers towards the end of that period.

The children begged for mercy and asked for strength to smile, leaving the majority of worshippers prostrating at home. Thus this led for Islam to stay alive as the children had a place to learn the lingualistic rules of recitation for prostration and engraved the desire to listen.

Most of all the children were encouraged to ask questions. Each question that was asked was returned with a comfortable reply. If the question faced a factual answer that couldn't be answered by a particular parent or practitioner, the child was given an honest alternative. "We don't know, best to ask someone who has studied in those facts for the most accurate answer." The elders were not ashamed if the question was unheard of before, as changing generations inevitably brought changed tasks. And unlike historical pasts, children were not mislead on prevailing the truth, just as adults would pause before lying on closed questions.

Moments for pray would become difficult especially when exploring into adulthood. Nevertheless a feeling of attraction was felt when standing on a pray mat when thousands of thousands of people pray. The feeling of attraction how man is drawn to water. The Son of God spoke of the Father, and thus the future as when to leave the left hand of God free. The attraction pulled when facing east not west is distinguishable. Some answers are too difficult to answer like, is the attraction due to the earth spinning counter-clockwise, west to east? Or does standing alone on faith exist? The answer becomes null when the question itself needs applauding upon merely for its existence.

Short sentences with counted pauses allowed pray to Allah where sound came before language. Fifteen laws held the faith for Allah to hear us. Following the fifteen laws became easier as they became pleasurable. The scriptures all fell into each other and tightened amongst themselves except for one law that contradicted the others.

Beautifully understood that this one reversed law, reversed within itself, and became blissful as the scratch was forgiven when recited from the Holy Qur'an. The sentence of sound was not to prostrate whilst scripture was being read.

The other fourteen laws embedded themselves within the children and into the twenty-second century which allowed more food to grow. Prostration was the key to life when away from holy words, prostration meaning to lie face down and touch the ground, total devotion towards repentance. To preach prostration draws close to Allah. We ask for joy so we can weep.

The sun or the moon with the earth and all of space not to be worshipped, but only Allah, Father, Creator, More, to be worshipped and worshipped alone. All those that worship Him will never fall in fire and would be given sights of respect by crows when Father pleased.

So people lost their pride in worshipping their clothes of sterling and praised the Lord. Either consciously or unconsciously they would bow their heads when their clothes were smudged, or when checking the time on their watches, or by playing with their phones. The quoted number was recited to prostrate ourselves, to do well, to pray with desire, and this all led to have knowledge of their successes.

Thus without pride, people came from all depths of the earth to kneel onto the ground that Allah had made. That all the shadows of the mornings and evenings bowed to Him, and sang holy, holy, holy allow us to prostrate beneath you.

The laws fill necessity to believe as much as Allah knows through time that most people would not. And those that do will end suffering for others. Others Allah will disgrace and those who were righteous can too be ignored, as too Allah will ignore those that ignored the righteous. Thus the disgraced dwell in Satan, dismissing that prostration is clearly to Allah and then thy neighbour. Hence to allow the disgraced find redemption if not given by their victim.

Time and time again, sound words to pauses to embed the weeping of Noah and Abraham before Allah. King David as he agreed to find repentance through the Lord, he found peace into salvation, that even without his son or his wealth Allah forgave him, and brought him closer to understanding that he knew nothing besides the will for him to write and enter heaven.

The shadows within the sight of Allah came to deliver another prophet to allow balance to be appreciated. He allowed the voices of the Holy Qur'an to be understood and be presented as hymns. These hymns were preached with joyful strength to the coming generations to keep the earth turning. Thus after the saviour left, the last prophet, Prophet Muhammad came and kept the fear in the Lord alive.

The differences in religion were only in environment as the atmosphere was exactly the same. Hence members of world religions had become one. Because you love us Father we can love. The power of love is like ephedrine.

Ephedrine evolved from an inspirational idea for the need to increase heart and breathing for a dying individual. The idea was like light or a sequence of lights that better made themselves the Light. A light illuminated itself as the creativity and eternal wellbeing of each and every living being. This Light was what everyone sentenced as one. Communities soon needed entertainment from the life they lived. Entertainment was anything considered 'cool', anything peaceful, anything casting a shadow or the horizon itself. Many horizons but holding peace still was cool and was something coloured black. Black was searched for when the Light approached fast or beamed too bright. So the circle of religion merged into one as they began to count the drops of ephedrine needed to mix with blood. Red was the colour of blood and the colour of love for blood. Overall people monopolized the unrequited love and made peace and real love as lightning.

XLV: Love & War
RED

All red cents had been shown to Tamana just before Christmas Day 2006. All the practice she had performed allowed her to have restraint on feeling emotion for her patients. Her apparel of scrubs was changed as often as inflammation would without a rectifying raconteur. In a single day she overcame a red streak towards the world's top causes of inherited and acquired death.

Autoimmune disease such as multiple sclerosis, rheumatoid arthritis, type I diabetes or vasculitis, initiated by the riddle of the body's own immune system attacking its own tissues, was what she declared to a few patients that day. As calm as a ladybug she rationalized treatment for those blowing raspberries and those souls' really suffering.

Immunosuppressant drugs are manufactured to be reflectively used in organ transplant patients. Some like azathioprine and cyclosporine are used to reduce inflammation from host immune activity, and those individuals' taking these medications are diagnosed with autoimmune conditions. Reciprocally these drugs would inhibit the patient's defense towards infection and may induce cancer. Tamana was to make the patients aware of this. Initially she prescribed prednisone; a corticosteroid, like all steroids have side effects, but hopefully with controlled doses they could respond without remorse.

The reaction of supplemental corticosteroids was to enhance the body's natural supply of steroid hormones produced by the adrenal cortex: the glucocorticoids (cortisol), and mineralocorticoids (aldosterone). Randomly these have been triggered off, and basic functions as fat, protein and carbohydrate metabolisms have become affected. Naturally the former controls basic metabolism, alongside limiting phospholipid build up in cells, the latter controls renal activity. Unfortunately the adrenal glands have become like raisins, that now the only hopeful cure would be to rely on a remedy that could alter a ribosome completely.

Consuming only a red apple for lunch Tamana walked onto the oncology floor. Least likely human cells had proliferated into metastasis by radiation therapy, but this she had to keep in mind especially when the individual had been forced to arrive. Most reliably the red herring was due to acquired habits, as excessive smoking and drinking, all rained over with ridiculous amounts of stress or random acts of love. Improve diet, improve lifestyle, and improve exercise, if all fails try immunosuppressants, try radiotherapy, try surgery, learn the ramble between a Summer Tanager and a Vermilion Flycatcher; and learn that repentance had to come from another.

Caution to the wind and share likely when a stop-sign octagon comes in sight. Both are careful as they take a right. The sign as a tomato to one person, and a red capsicum bell pepper to another, made no sense when Tamana heard she would have to give a red ribbon to an infant.

In contrast to an autoimmune disease, acquired immunodeficiency syndrome, is presented by a virus that affects lymphatic cells not to respond to infections, primarily affecting the brain, the retinas, the lungs, the skin and the gastrointestinal tract. The only rapport of the virus was to prevent the infected from living and breeding. The only human cure was to begin to live life healthily and peacefully. Antiviral therapy inhibits reverse transcriptase activity of the virus forming more viral-RNA, which slows down the rascal development of painful infectious and malignant deaths. Best to either be courteous about one's own life or that given to others, providing that the resistant vaccine was available.

Tamana's heart grew to be overwhelmed to see the infant smile. Royally she saved her tears and walked to wash and change. Retiring out of the evening and hopefully for Christmas Day she made her way out of the hospital. She dodged a stretcher entering the emergency room heading straight to surgery. The person was trying to be resuscitated. There did not seem to be any lesions on him, or any cuts, or bruises. The man was large, the man ate red meat excessively, the man drank excessively, the man was a reduplicate of another and the man needed a cardiac shock as the other.

XLVI: Love & War
RED

Relying on keeping the raging bull of all men's needs to fall baron at bay, the time-traveler had to be well aware not to encounter trouble as he traveled. Derrick had to study the cries of war that the people of earth had to suffer to make his home a safer place to live, and his vacations a safer place to visit.

Cries from murder in the twentieth century fell all upon race, and drafts of ethnicity, or communism. If one cry came from one person to kill the unjust then his word would be questioned, even though he sat by the right hand of God. A rancor for racial blood to be spilt was more appreciated amongst the nitwits that relied on race to be the only reason to murder.

Initially the stories of crusades building empires that led to millions to die by the knife. In 1914, World War I horned for people to find shelter against the resistance of Russian communism, that after four years and three months found armistice. The Russian Revolution being the world's first communist change from Tsarist Monarchy, led to the bloodshed of the monarchy in

1918. Now these random acts of violence left red on sand and snow.

A massive turn of events from World War I, not only caused no travel to New York, Wall Street, but also stopped ranches being built on free land in 1929. Widespread bankruptcy to unemployment resulted in no place to raise cattle; the only place to work was back to war and stop Nazis' making genocide of the Jewish in World War II. And stop Hitler's fascist movement. Six million Jews murdered and rivers were to run red blood, but some Jews were burnt instead.

Luckily the atomic bomb was created that stopped the war, by killing only a mare 160,000 in 1945. Benefit of the mushroom shaped out blast was so no rivers ran septic as the blood of the victims' was immediately vaporized to air.

Ransacking with new rifles gave ideas to the state of Israel concluding World War II in 1948. Palestine wanting freedom to live as an independent nation, but pressures from Arabia and Israel, remixed with pet fights, would carry on until there was nobody there to nourish the land. The land would become dry and not even vultures would land to feed. Pity was by far out of reach for those people. The answer was simple; the nation with the most wealth upon feeding and providing shelter for the state, should have taken complete remodeling of the coastal state of Israel. Not one individual had worked hard to keep what they had built, but all kept fighting to destroy little of what they had left. All prays across that park to remain holy, but now there's only one pray to silence them altogether. One ranger could take care of that park; the people should appreciate that ranger.

The countdown for Armageddon during 1962 Cuban Missile Crisis allowed closure of the Cold War. For people to recognize that stools were prepared the same way regardless to where they lived was harder to imagine than the clock that had stopped ticking, and had shut close the gates of heaven. The fortunate should learn to provide a whole lot better. As its fair to say what was taken from the Red-Indians could still be taken from the Americans. Rubies can be exchanged for robins, and the feet of the young for the heart of the elders.

There will always be a fortunate and someone left to neglect. Rotating this concentration will still make no sense, but finding a narrow pivot would ridiculously balance the love. Just like the Iranian Revolution in 1979, that only living for ignorance of one's own kind would make finest rituals for Allah to weep.

Through the pages of repeated history many have come to rise and many had regressed into suffrage and poverty. Realizing that had made the rich humble to the poor respectful they brought roses to be thrilled in their standing.

Pleased as some had come to flatten tyranny of evil, some as Jay-Z to Aamir Khan would and could bring destruction from a moments glance; nevertheless they obey the Father's request to give love instead, to shine their light. Leaving morals of pray to be taken harshly, if not to play sports aggressively, stop the hilarious types of bloodshed supposedly, or nobody would have retired from dying out of the starring towers for eternity.

XLVII: Love & War
RED

The range between January 21st and February 20th declares the start of the Spring Festival in China, also known as Chinese New Year. The lunisolar Chinese calendar relies on the wait of the second new moon after the winter solstice to mark the beginning of spring. The Chinese come to rejoice in this occasion for fifteen days. Derrick and Tamana came to join in their festivities in the year of the rabbit in 2011.

Beijing was decorated with candles, lanterns, celebrated with dragon dances, small firecrackers, and all enjoying fine cuisines from noodles to sweet glutinous rice balls in soup. The first day was to welcome deities of heaven to bring warm prospects for the following year. Families would visit the elders, and the married folk would give youngsters red paper envelopes filled with money. Tamana honored the Chinese ritual upon honoring family members with those alive or deceased that they prayed with them, and they prayed for a family of their own.

"What's on the cards for the people of the world Des?" she asked Derrick, whilst lighting a

191

candle for the Jade Emperor of Heaven, as the Chinese do on the ninth day.

"I like to say that if the right receptors are triggered then the people of the world will prosper greatly," he replied whilst staring at the lit flame.

"After removing all the rebels, raids and rafter from history, where shall we focus our attention?" she said, as very well she knew that Derrick had seen much further in the future.

"What has brought all this on?" he returned.

Trying to hide her emotions that she could not share with the people around her, and hiding under her gorgeous figure that curved her cherry dress she cried: "Just answer me. What do we need to do to keep this light shining?"

"You almost blew your candle out. Very well I think there are many raffling ethics intertwined like a dismantled rubric in the world. I agree that Buddhists and others have rituals on not eating meat products on some days, but can the world really argue on genetically modified organisms, helping to grow quantity and quality food for increasing populations? Secondly, if population growth doesn't slow down we are to look for new forms of energy other than nuclear and oil. There are hydrogen cars, hydro-electric power stations, with solar and wind electric generators as well, but not following closely to the Kyoto Protocol by the United Nations, the world's leading countries are going to cause a massive effect on global warming, and unfortunately these are going to be hard to reverse," Derrick blinked four times. "And do you really want to know what would happen after this? I say 'would' as if people ruled out a few points of personal ethics then this light will always keep shining."

"He has written in Romans 1:20 that 'there's no excuse not to learn.' We should learn as a fox not to allow others to step into danger. The healthcare systems in the world are a good example of this. Simple basic diseases as malaria and flu due to contamination of water or lack of diet, millions of paramedics that can respond to millions of doctors, in turn can bring millions of people vaccines. How do high levels of healthcare insurance make sense? Take Heath Ledger for example, it's worse now than before we had penicillin," he paused so Tamana could realize that he was not talking about her specifically.

"All I'm trying to say is that not all people have to be born to breed. And if they are to breed, then they to be fully aware for whom they are multiplying for. Use genetic intervention, use embryonic stem cell research, safely, appropriately and allow people to appreciate that form of curing diseases and aborting babies. People forget that they should live for the Lord's love when they supposedly lose something or work without

193

reward. I pray for ramification amongst individuals to either make no decision or make the right one," Derrick stepped back to admire Tamana. "We'll have three, lovely and as radiant as you."

Tamana pressed up against Derrick and placed his hands on her hips, "Tonight," she declared, and moved her lips to his ears, "General."

The 'General' she was remarking to be was General Guan Yu who was honored by the Chinese on the thirteenth day of festivities. General Guan Yu was acknowledged for his truthfulness, loyalty and strength over hundred raptorial riots for the Emperor.

XLVIII: Love & War
RED

Reproducing had benefited in some scenarios. Red roses bloomed to show affection for the emotion of love, and their beauty resembled cures for the depressed. Rewards in history as such marked the time-traveler to assess adventure as greatly as a conducted copper wire. The energy from reverting his thoughts of histories past failures allowed Derrick to appreciate what had been successfully conquered.

For instance the first printed book being the Gutenberg Bible in Mainz, Germany, on 23rd February 1455. Before this, kingdoms had chambers called scriptoriums where scholars would sit day and night replicating scripture.

Anesthesia was a huge hurdle that was overcome. The production of cocaine from the leaves of the coca plant administered in safe doses allowed for anesthesia to animal nerve systems. From 1884 the effects of this plant had helped hundreds of surgeons perform operations with reliance on comfort. In 1904 an aminoester form of the local anesthetic was formulated as procaine, and throughout the last century clinical trials have improved the action of the agent, allowing for a miracle ease for relieving pain.

The Coca-Cola Company, established in 1886 began to provide bursts of energy to mostly everyone on the globe. Derrick enjoyed the recipe from this soda compared to that of others, possibly for the high content of cocaine prepared from coca leaf and caffeine prepared from the kola nut. A mixture of this drink with plain water provided enough energy and nourishment to bodily cells to accomplish any task.

In 1914, Emmeline Pankhurst, led the Women's Suffrage out of redemption by chaining herself to the bars of Buckingham Palace. She notably was arrested, but she gave spice as strong as a red chili to allow women's right to vote from 1928. The era was one to be admired by Preity Zinta, and Tamana; however Derrick had no interest in placing either of them close to the ramblings.

Another turn in history that inspired Derrick to achieve his own was when he read about Deoxyribonucleic Acid (DNA), found by Watson and Crick in 1953, a double helix series of nucleotides that coded for the genetic makeup of organisms. The remarkable breakthrough in biochemical engineering that allowed genotypes of cellular functions to be analyzed. Fifty years later the Human Genome Project was complete, the sequence of genes within chromosomes was complete. These sequences could not only provide a template for an ideal growth of a human, but also to distinguish humans from Red-tailed Hawks, flamingos, strawberries, raspberries, Flaming Red Oaks and other non-synthetic things.

Just as for every man gave his rib for each woman; possibly for affection or possibly for stem cells; the freedom of speech for all individuals was declared when Martin Luther King, Jr. of the United States, met Mahatma Gandhi of India, in 1959. This in turn empowered the Civil Rights Movement to eradicate racial segregation. The famous "I have a dream" speech was one to be reckoned with, and Derrick asked Tamana if she'd like to visit Washington D.C. on 28th August 1963. She agreed.

The travel to the moon in 1969 was well appreciated by the thousand minds at NASA, recounting that not one man was to be praised, but instead one devotion.

Love was not just accounted for by technology alone; the moonwalk of Michael Jackson in Wembley 1988, across the Bad concert was another remembrance of how people felt when standing together.

A little later just as thousand minds knocked down the Berlin Wall in 1989 to bring an end to repining death, Tim Berners-Lee brought multitudes of awareness to thousand minds across the globe, through the world-wide-web in 1991.

Further still ringing of radio waves brought better communication to use digital medium of electro-modulated waves to signal telephonic wi-fi into the twenty-first century. And as for Derrick the turnouts of thankful revolution allowed him to look forward upon his prays for revelation.

XLIX: Finale
BLACK

Wellbeing of their nature for one another grew to greater depths as time drifted. The friends began exploring different eras every time the earth turned to colder weathers in Moscow. Together they traveled around the world exploring what countries had to offer around the clock. The countries they had past time with became their excuse to stay closer to Derrick. Tribute given to Derrick as he had already witnessed the loss of his friends and so they trailed close to witness themselves the drop of his tears. Through the cloudy days of most in Moscow, Derrick decided that he should leave.

Blackthorn winter had approached with the white flowers of the thorny shrub about to blossom with the dark berries for the new cold season. Like all travels that the friends had listed prior to this one began in Dormition Cathedral. Lighting candles for those that indefinitely lived in darkness; museums clerks, librarians, repenting prisoners, homeless souls, overworked physicians, and soldiers that built hospitals in the line of combat, all the bone thugs playing to harmony, and so they gave thanks for their blessings that had been provided for them. The friends dipped their fingers in the hallow service of holy water into the cathedral.

From outside the cathedral was life working to keep the walls of faith safe. Children playing along with sirens' howling like wolves could be heard simultaneously. Sirens molted within white falling snow that embedded the emergency vehicles could only be seen as flashes of strobe in the best of circumstances. The dusky gloom atmosphere of night Moscow with falling snow made these drivers the best of their kind not to skid. The roads by far became covered overnight that during day settled snow turned to slippery ice sludge. To keep all things blackened from the blinding snow so the sirens could be heard throughout Moscow also required the application of sand and salt.

Inside the cathedral the choir brushed their gowns and waited for the choir leader to begin the hymns during ceremony. Ceremonies presented themselves to establish the new world, that world presented by Christ for the forgiveness of all sins, past, present and future, for Christ to present himself with name to stand as 'Jesus is Lord'.

The friends stood close to the middle row left to the speaker's sight. Abraham was to the far left, Derrick stood by Abraham's left and Tamana alongside with him, leaving Craig beside her, and

Tyler by the aisle closest to the foot of the cross. The choir began with psalms; the friends listened in and enjoyed their environment. They stood, sometimes with hands together, sometimes as stance, sometimes as pose using the dark wood back rest of the row ahead with the forefinger.

Leaning back Derrick bowed his head to the floor and then to a donation envelope, to a book, to the wood of the seating, through the clear black spaces of rows ahead of him, to a dark shadow on the altar resting ahead of Derrick. A spider crawled out from behind a candle stand on the altar and dashed over towards Derrick's sight making Abram startle. The spider stood for a moment then dashed over the ledge behind the altar's offering.

The surprising thing about that the friends found was, why had the spider come to the light during service? Without any auditory senses the spider was not prone to hearing the music. The only possibility that they could ponder was that the spider could feel the vibrations of notes off the walls of the building, that the spider came to see. Slightly startled Abram opened his mouth so the insect would not come any closer and groaned alongside with the choir.

Prays were followed by the end of the service. Prays to signify a prosperous start to 2011, and prays to bring Derrick's friends to realization and move away from him. Derrick nudged Abram and moved in-between Tamana's toes, pass Craig, to Tyler and out to the aisle. They blinked and watched their friend sit in the first row closest to the foot of the cross. Derrick bowed his head and pressed his hands together towards a mounted nailed person on a crucifix.

He began tapping his first fingers together for several seconds and then held them. He held them a little longer and allowed the rest of his fingers to touch. His friends began to feel uncomfortable. They had witnessed Derrick moving his pray into his world before, and every time they would fall to wish he was pretending to do his nails. They glanced over at Tamana, she was in pray into her palms, and she smiled gently bringing her palms closer to her face. She looked up close at her palms as the others moved to their brother.

Abram walked over his left down the rows minding the people leaving the building. He pardoned his stride just to be observant of Derrick's thoughts. Craig moved Tyler out onto the aisle and stepped him down towards the second row. They smiled graciously as elders, seniors, adults, adolescents, toddlers, and choir members as they move to provide donations and final condolences. Tamana walked down to a few rows behind them and sat in a right row of the sight from the foot of the cross.

For the protection and immunity for Derrick's wellbeing he remained bowed on his seat. He began with soft prays that could be heard by the friends as slow whispers. The whispers gradually absorbed the light radiating from him to fall upon his friends. The discreet secret that Derrick whispered amongst the Father filled air into the lungs of his friends. Three hands touched gently the shoulders of Derrick and pressured him not to stand. They stood there in silence revealing their love to their friend. His lungs filled with air and he expanded his brawn. Gradually as young birds leaving their nest, Abram, Tyler and Craig left Derrick in Amen. They left their deeper than blood brother in peace with the Lord and followed their own light.

L: Finale
BLACK

Continuously the rain fell throughout the day. The clouds had thickened for the past week that they could not contain themselves any longer. As soon as the earth had revolved from night, enough for the sunrays to approach Moscow from the east, the streets began to become cooled by the storm brewing from the west. The weather forecast for the evening was to have the raindrops change to snowflakes. Evening approached and the rain had stopped.

From the horizon opposite the entrance to the New Opera Theatre over the telephone cable lines a raven soared. The rest of the rain allowed the people below to look above at the raven circling into a helix towards the ground. A soul of prey that was made accustomed to bow during all times of the day. Nevertheless the people looked about their way and the only one watching the people was the raven. He descended with stretched wings to perch on the roof of the theatre.

As the bird of prey stepped foot onto the building he folded his wings and cried a caw three times. Chasing behind his laugh followed screaming police sirens, and their laugh that resonated throughout the city streets around Pushkinskaya Metro, and up towards the sky immediately filled the sky with snow. The snow fell softly with large snowflakes and began covering horizons like remnants of volcanic ash.

Streetlights began to switch on allowing the falling snow to be seen by Moscow habitants. The snow became entrapped with a warm wind that made them dance under the streetlights. The streetlights lit cafés where clean aprons were worn everyday serving black coffee. Black coffee seemed that much richer as individuals began to make themselves comfortable within the cold. The cold air was slowly being pushed away for the night from the city, to the seas; pass the suburban and rural areas of miners. Coal miners and iron workers packed their tools to make haste on reaching home before the blizzards trapped them to work for longer. Wind chilled to the core stretched with frost that howled through the shivering souls out from the metros of Moscow cooled the raven to rest. More streetlights switched on.

"Beautifully, sing it to me, where we go from here? Shall I pack my bags? Shall I wear my shoes? Oh, who knows but you? I don't know, nor does Cain, what I've done to my brothers, along the way. Oh, you cry more, if we're last for sure, how can I not switch you on?" sang Derrick.

Within the New Opera Theatre, staring at the light that reflected off the table sat Derrick singing to distract himself from his thought of work. Once he came to realization that he was sidetracked he found his black cube that he used as a paperweight on his table, and brought himself out of the light. Staring at anything black would have helped, nevertheless he liked to make the most simplest of things exciting, so he sat and stared at the cube and brought himself to thought.

"Electromagnetic 'EM' waves consist of radiowaves, microwaves, infrared 'IR' rays, visible 'ROY G BIV' rays, ultraviolet light, X-rays and gamma-rays. Speed of light from Maxwell's equations between electric and magnetic forces allows light waves to travel when $c = 3 \times 10^8$m/s. Properties of EM waves travel perpendicular to each other. Everything is checked including the radiation pressures of the invisible waves that travel through space or power cables that ensure harnessing the energy can be stable. Electrical force over magnetic force, $E/B = c$ brings me to control the speed of travel with a window variable of 100 m/s." dictated Derrick to himself and gave a large sigh.

Weighing himself within the heat of his basement away from the rest of the chilled filled theatre, Derrick made preparations to test his invention. Derrick hesitated each time he held the titanium-carbon coated time-machine. He propped his device to balance still on the ground with his left hand and hesitated again. He queried if he should represent the white pieces or the dark pieces of a battle chess set. Neither of which would make a difference to his overall task to see if his invention would work or not. Dropping the staff onto his couch he grabbed a pencil and began to scribble off sheets of carbon graphite as lead onto blank pieces of paper.

Outside of his lair, there was a thud at the door, loud enough for Derrick to hear but he had not. Music beating through large amplifiers masqueraded a break in. The concentration between anxiety and curiosity blinded Derrick to witness that someone had entered his lair. The heavy weight of space that shrank around his own habitat made him stand. He walked over to his couch and picked up the time-machine.

The break-in was caused by a stranger of Moscow. The stranger overwhelmed with the free entrance, and bewildered from the cold, along with the loud music springing his hangover allowed him to keep his knife sheathed. This stranger was Craig Goncharov He paced softly to the door where the music was coming from. All of a sudden there was loud tuned note sang from the opposite side.

Desperation marked the stranger as one victim, instead of two and waited. One shadow distorted the beam of light from under the doorway for several seconds. There came another note of the same pitch from the other side of the door. The stranger waited several seconds and turned the doorknob and stepped into his victim's blind spot. Nothing was going to stop his hunger than himself.

Derrick paced himself to the wall furthest from the door and smacked his hanging fighter bag with his right thenar eminence, hard, and rattattatat, rattattat, he exploded on his fighter bag with a mixture of push into stances, with eminences and sidekicks, back side sick, rattatat-attack, tat, tat, until he pushed his whole body into the bag, pushing his force out of the back of the bag, and hugged the bag one time to stand still. He slowly paced himself back where the light was shining off his notes. Pushing his fingertips together he tensed his whole body, extraction of his quadriceps to push his thumbs along with supporting his back to brawn to stance. Derrick stared at the time-machine and sat down.

Shortening his stride stepped out of the shadows the stranger. The stranger unsheathed his weapon. He moved down the landing into the right shoulder of his victim. Derrick stood abruptly pushing his chair back to block the stranger closer. The stranger moved behind the victim, behind the wall of his kitchen and watched him move to the living space of his area. Derrick lifted the time-machine as a swordsman offering his weapon to a king that the stranger was clueless on what to do.

Craig walked closer to his victim as he adjusted to his own thought. Derrick twirled the time-machine to stop in both hands. Derrick had quietly grabbed his grip of his device and pushed a surface of the device to begin harnessing power. Through the change of reflection of light off the surface of the casing of the time-machine, he noticed he wasn't alone. The stranger leaned in to grab the contraption away from his victim's hands. Pushing the weight barrier of chance Derrick pushed himself back into the light, and pushed the assaulter off guard. Derrick shrunk his brawn and pushed up to strike the stranger, and whilst watching him fall to his mercy the time-machine had powered. Derrick noticed a deep scratch that was leaking on his invention and threw the time-machine onto the couch. He grabbed the assaulter and moved him into the kitchen; pulling open the pantry Derrick threw himself and the Craig in like he was throwing trash into a trash bin. A large explosion forced the door to shut.

The raven that sat above the theatre felt the concrete of his ledge halt. Without waiting any longer to find cause or effect he lifted his brawn and stretched straight out up into the falling snow.

Everything within the building, from the basement to the theatre lobby, all the floors, with all the cushions, and the stage with the curtains were torn to splinters and splits in thread, and what wasn't was on fire in a matter of seconds. There was no light to shine into the pantry, and the pantry had no need for a safety light if one knew where the handle fit. Through all possibilities everything stayed alive. Through all necessities the earth stopped trembling. Through all realities the pantry door pushed open.

Epilogue

There once was an American man, an English man, an Indian man, an Islamic man, a Hispanic man, a European man, an Oriental man, an Australian man and an African man, they were all in a helicopter flying over the River Nile.

The American man lights a cigarette and then throws it out onto the world. The others ask him why he did that? And he replied, "I'll make more on my land."

The English man cracks open a can of ale and then throws it out onto the world. The others ask him why he did that? And he replied, "I'll brew more on my land."

The Indian man peels a banana and throws it out onto the world. The others ask him why he did that? And he replied, "I'll plant more on my land."

The Islamic man breaks his pray beads and throws them out onto the world. The others ask him why he did that? He replied, "I have more on my land."

The Hispanic man picks up his gun and throws it out onto the world. The others ask him why he did that? And he replied, "I'll buy more on my land."

The European man pulls out a book and throws it out onto the world. The others ask him why he did that? He replied, "I'll print another on my land."

The Oriental man looks at his videogame and throws it out onto the world. The others ask him why he did that? And he replied, "I'll create another from my land."

The African man stands up and throws the American man, English man, Indian man, Islamic man, Hispanic man, European man and the Oriental man out onto the world. The Australian man asks him why he did that? And he replies, "I'm tired of them littering on my land."

The Australian man shook the African man's hand.

Works Citied

About.com. (2009). Cooking Terms - K. <southernfood.about.com/library/info/bld_k.htm>

Abrams, Jim. (2008). Congress bucks Bush on Medicaid. The Greenville News. P.10A. 04/24/08.

Ahmad Damir. (1999-2009). Islamonline.net. Moscows okays Construction of New Mosque. <http://www.islamonline.net/English/News/2004-05/26/article06.shtml>

Alhajji, A.F. Williams, James L. (02/02/03). Coming Energy Crisis? Energy Economics Newsletter. <http://www.wtrg.com/EnergyCrisis/index.html> Retrieved 2/4/2008.

Amrikee, Abu Y A. (2006). Islam Uncovered. Glossary (Commonly used terms by Muslims). <islamuncovered.com/terminologies/terms.htm>

AnaesthesiaUK. (04/03/2005). Cannulation of antecubital veins. <www.frca.co.uk/article.aspx?articleid=100034>

ARD. (2005). The common agricultural policy – A glossary of terms. Agricultural and Rural Development. (10 Oct 2005). <ec.europa.eu/agriculture/glossary/index_en.htm>

Asia.ru. (2006-2008). Russia. <http://travel.asia.ru/travel2russia/russia/information/document2936.shtml>

Bernstein J.A., Bernstein I.L., Bucchini L., Goldman L.R., Hamilton R.G., Lehrer S., Rubin C., and Sampson H.A. (2003). Clinical and laboratory investigation of allergy to genetically modified foods. Environmental Health Perspectives, 111(8), 1114-1121.

Big Ideas that Changed the World. (10/29/2007). Events that Changed Our World. <http://www.mymultiplesclerosis.co.uk/big-ideas/change-events.html>

Bohin, Ray. Genetic Intervention: The Ethical Challenges Ahead. The Center for Bioethics and Human Dignity. 2000. <http://www.cbhd.org/resources/genetics/bohlin_2000-04-07_print.htm>

Booking.com. (2009). Marriott Moscow Royal Aurora. <http://www.booking.com/hotel/ru/marriott-moscow-royal-aurora.html>

Booking.com. (2009). 9 Hotels near Khodynka Arena. <http://www.booking.com/searchresults.html>

Bruce, Donald. (2007). Cloning and Stem Cells. Society, Religion and Technology Project. Church of Scotland <srtp.org.uk/cloning.shtmal>

Brunswick. (2004). Hobocmu.

Bush. (2008). 2008 State of the Union. January 29, 2008). Whitehouse.gov.

Bush, President. George. W. (2005). President signs Energy Policy Act. The White House. <http://www.whitehouse.gov/news/releases/2005/08/20050808-6.html> Retrieved April 26, 2008.

Bush, George. (2001). The White House. President Discusses Stem Cell Research. Texas. <http://www.whitehouse.gov/news/releases/2001/08/20010809-2.html> Retrieved April 25, 2008.

Cambell, Mike. (1996-2009). Behind the Name. Russian Names. <http://www.behindthename.com/nmc/rus.php>

Carr, C.T. Coulson, J. Eagle, Dorothy. Hutchinson, Lucy. (1962). The Oxford Illustrated Dictionary. Oxford University Press.

Charles Colson and Nigel Cameron, editors. (2004). Biotic and Public Policy. The European Debate. Human Dignity in the Biotech Century. Intervarsity Press, 2004.

Cioc, Mark. Millar, Char. Showers, Kate eds. (1999). "Regulation of Nuclear-Power Plants in the United States." History in Dispute, Vol. 7: Water and the Environment Since 1945: Global Perspectives. St. James Press. Reproduced in History Resource Center. Farmington Hills, MI: Gale. <galenet.galegroup.com/servlet/HistRC/>

Clark, Jimmy. (Apr. 25. 2001). No Significant Difference Found in Animals Fed GMO Corn and Soybeans. Aces News. University of Illinois. <http://www.aces.uiuc.edu/news/stories/news137 4.html> Retrieved April 25, 2008.

Collins, Francis S. (2006). The Language of God. A scientist presents evidence for belief. NY.

Cryptogenic Organising Pneumonitis. (12/18/2006). Prednisone & prednisolone steroid use & its potential side-effects on patients. <cop-boop.org.uk/steroid_use_&_effects.htm>

Cummings, Benjamin. (2001). Addison Wesley Longham Inc. Right Leg Muscles. <octc.kctcs.edu/gcaplan/anat/images/Image404>

Dan Perushev. (2001-2003). Way to Russia. Russian Food and Cuisine – Everything about Traditional Food in Russia and Authentic Russian Recipes. <

Department of Work and Pensions (DWP). (2008).
Terms and Abbreviations. England.
<http://www.dwp.gov.uk/advisers/z1/terms.asp>
Retrieved April 24, 2008.

Domodedovo Moscow International Airport. (2002-2009). Flight Schedules.
<domodedovo.ru/en/main/timetablenew/>

Donkor, Stephen Maxwell. (05/03/2009). UN
Water/Africa (IGWA). The African Water
Facility is Operational.
<uneca.org/awich/AWF/Announcement.htm>

Encarta. msn. (2009). Top 10 World-Changing Events.
<http://uk.encarta.msn.com/encnet/features/lists/?article=WorldEvents>

English Russia. (2009). The Moscow Mosque.
<http://englishrussia.com/?p=1898>

Environmental Ethics Reading. GMO. Genetically
Modified Organisms. The Complex Difficult.
Frankenfood.
<https://mycampus.swu.edu/ics/Academics/BIOL/BIOL_3313/2007_20-BIOL_3313-0001/>
Retrieved April 25 2008.

"Ethics". Encyclopedia Britannica. (2008).
Encyclopedia Britannica Online. March 15, 2008.
<britannica.com/eb/article-252572/ethics>

Evans. C.T. (2000).1998 Muhammad Ali.
<http://novaonline.nvcc.edu/eli/evans/his135/events/ali98.htm>

Fogt, Robert. (1997-2008). Women's Shoe Size
Conversion. Welcome to OnlineConversion.com.
<onlineconversion.com/clothing_shoes_womens.htm>

Gavin, Raewyn, Dr. (04/08). Morphine Administration.
<http://www.starship.org.nz/Clinical%20Guidelin
e%20PDFs/Morphine%20Administration.pdf>

Geographi. (2009). Russian geography –Regions of
Russia.
<russianembassy.org/RUSSIA/geograf.htm>

Get a huge tank.com (2009). Indigo Hemlet.
<getahugetank.com/indigo-hamlet-p-380.html>

Gilland, Ben. (05/01/2009). Science and Discovery.
MetroCosm. Metro. The rise of the little people.
P18-19. <http://img.metro.co.uk/e-edition>

Gobal, Paul. (11/26/2008). Windowoneurasia. Window
on Eurasia: A Saudi Mosque in Moscow in
Exchange for a Russian Church in Mecca?
<http://windowoneurasia.blogspot.com/2008/11/
window-on-eurasia-saudi-mosque-in.html>

Godzillas. (05/12/2010). Moscow Metro Map.
[godzillashostel.com/images/maps/metromap.gif]

Goldberg, Daniella. (2008). Cloning Around with Stem
Cells. ABC Science Online.
<abc.net.au/science/slab/stemcells/default.htm>

Google Maps. (03/19/2009). Hospitals near Russian
Federation, Moscow.

Google Maps. (2009). Moscow. [maps.google.com]

Healthcare Economist. (Feb 4, 2008). Should the NHS
pay for medical procedures for smokers and the
elderly. <http://healthcare-economist.com>

Henkel AG & Co. (04/27/2007). Henkel Sponsors Ice
Hockey World Cup in Russia.
<henkel.com/cps/rde/xchg/SID-0AC8330A-
5B.htm>

Hursthouse, Rosalind. (Jul 18 2008). Virtue Ethics. Stanford Encyclopedia of Philosophy. Stanford University. CA. Metaphysics Research Lab. <science.uva.nl/~seop/entries/ethics-virtue/>

IBS-STL Global. (2008). Introductions to the Books of the Bible. <ibsstl.org/niv/studybible/index.php>

Javins, Marie. (05/17/2001). Party bus to Bukhara. <mariesworldtour.com/entries/0518.html>

Kamal, Mohammad Rashid. (06/28/2009). Saudi Gazette, Arab translators and Islam's golden era. <http://www.saudigazette.com.sa/index.cfm?method=home.regcon&contentID=2008081514476>

Khaira, H.S. 10/28/2004. Anatomy of leg arteries.

King Fahd Complex For The Printing Of The Holy Qur'an. (02.04.2009). Qur'an Glossary. <http://qurancomplex.org/quran/mostalhat.asp?TablD=1&SubltemlD=8&I=eng>

Kolmogorov Conference. (03/15/2009). SightSeeing in Moscow. <kolmogorov-100.mi.ras.ru/info5.htm>

Krumboltz Mike. (03/17/2009). Meeta Maria Sergeyeva. <buzz.yahoo.com/buzzlog/92382>

Kyoto Protocol. (2005). Negotioating the Protocol. UNFCCC.int. <http://unfccc.int/kyoto_protocol/items/2830.php> Retrieved April 26, 2008.

Lemoine, N.R. Kirby, R.B. (2003). UK cash for gene therapy: Government pledges support. Gene therapy (2003). UK. <http://www.nature.com/gt/journal/v10/n17/full/3302119a.html> Retrieved on April 24, 2008.

Levine, Carol. (2006). Bioethics and Public Policy. 11th edition. McGrew Hill.

London. Scraps of Moscow. (02/2009).
    <www.scrapsofmoscow.org/2005/01/underground
    -moscow-6-chekhovskaya.html>
Lucas, Aykroyd. (06/05/2007). Straight.com. Moscow
    takes you back in the USSR.
    <http://www.straight.com/article-98028/moscow-
    takes-you-back-in-the-ussr>
Merck. (1995-2009). Autoimmune Disorders.
    <http://www.merck.com/mmhe/sec16/ch186/ch18
    6a.html#sec16-ch186-ch186a-280>
Moscow-Taxi.com. (2001-2007). Moscow Zoo.
    <moscow-taxi.com/4children/moscow-zoo.html>
Munson, Ronald. (2003). "Outcome
    Uncertain" Bioethics and Public Policy.
    Thompson-Wadsworth.
Munson, Ronald (2003). "Outcome Uncertain" Ethical
    Theories and Outcome of Medical Resources.
    Thompson-Wadsworth.
MyTravelGuide. (1999-2009). Jumah Mosque, South
    Africa. <mytravelguide.com/attractions/profile-
    79573205-
    South_Africa_Durban_Jumah_Mosque.html>
Nascar. (2001-2010). Nascar. Turner Sports Interactive,
    Inc. <http://www.nascar.com/>
Netter Frank. (2003). Atlas of Human Anatomy, 3rd
    Edition.<pitt.edu/~regional/Airway%20Blocks/Ai
    rwayPicture2.jpg>
Numan, Fareed, H. (December 1992). Islam101. The
    Muslim Population in the United States. "A Brief
    Statement." American Muslim Council.
    <http://www.islam101.com/history/population2_u
    sa.html>

Oceans Reefs and Aquariums. (2007). Fish – Indigo
    Dottyback. (03/22/2009).
    <http://www.orafarm.com/dottybacks.html>
Paranyshkin Dmitri, Smith Celina, Perushev Dan.
    (2002-2004). Way to Russia.
    <waytorussia.net/Moscow/Transport.html>
Propp DA, "Fixed vs. Variable Costs of Hospital Care"
    JAMA August 18, 1999; Vol. 282(7):630.
Propp, Douglas. A. (1999). Macroeconomics of
    Healthcare. Chicago.
ProZ – The translation workplace. (1999-2009).
    Natasha.
    <http://www.proz.com/kudoz/russian_to_english/l
    inguistics/712725-natasha.html>
Rawl, John. (September 3, 2002). A Theory of Justice.
    Harvard University Press, 1971.
    <www.wku.edu/~jan.garrett/ethics/johnrawl.htm>
RE: Quest Churches. (2007). Glossary of Tech' Words.
    [request.org.uk/main/churches/glossary.htm]
Ria Novosti. (08/06/2007). June 12 – Day of Russia.
    <en.rian.ru/symbols/20070608/66883669.html>
Rick Steves. (1998). Moscow, Russia.
    <www.ricksteves.com/plan/destinations/east/mos
    cow.htm>
Rindels, Sherry. (04/06/1994). Iowa State University.
    Horticulture & Home Pest News. Lettuce
    Varieties.
    <http://www.ipm.iastate.edu/ipm/hortnews/1994/
    4-6-1994/kinds.html>
Russian News & Information Agency, Novosti.
    (05/19/2008). Russia wins 2008 World

Championship in Canada.
<en.rian.ru/sports/20080519/107753003.html>

Russia Profile.org. (04/05/09). Moscow.
<http://www.russiaprofile.org/resources/territory/
districts/moscow/index.wbp>

Sacred Destinations. (2005-2009). St. Basil's
Cathedral, Moscow. <http://www.sacred-
destinations.com/russia/moscow-st-basil-
cathedral.htm>

Sbarro. (2006). Spirito dell' Italia!
<http://www.sbarro.ru/>

Shifrin, Tash. (Feb 6 2004). Government reveals NHS
price list. News. Guardian.co.uk. England.
<http://www.guardian.co.uk/society/2004/feb/06/
nhs2000.politics> Retrieved on April 24 2008.

Smith, Anne M. Wardlaw, Gorden M. 2007.
Contemporary Nutrition 6 ed. New York. Higher
Education. The McGraw-Hill Companies.

Smith, S.E. (2003-2009). Wise Geek. What was the
First Printed Book?
<http://www.wisegeek.com/what-was-the-first-
printed-book.htm>

Southan Michelle. (09/2006). Taste.com. Creamy
bacon and mushroom fettuccine.
<http://www.taste.com.au/recipes/8265/creamy+b
acon+mushroom+fettuccine>

St. Basil's Cathedral. (2007-2010).
WorldGreatestSites.com.
<http://www.worldgreatestsites.com/st_basils_cat
hedral.htm>

St. Petersburg Russia. (2009). Baltika Beer (Baltica
Beer). <bravosolutions.com/baltika_beer.php>

Taylar, Ingrid. (2009). About.com: San Francisco. Photos of California Coastal Birds. <http://sanfrancisco.about.com/od/sanfranciscophoto1/ig/californiabirds/>

The Amerisc Corp. (2008). Glossary. New York. <http://www.theamerisc.com/glossary_m.htm.> Retrieved April 24 2008.

The Moscow City Government. (2005-2009). The Moscow City Executive authorities. <http://www.mos.ru>

The New York Times. (10/22/1882). Humming Insects. <http://query.nytimes.com/mem/archive-free/pdf>

The Prayer Guide. (17/04/2009). The Lord's Prayer. <http://www.prayerguide.org.uk/lordsprayer.htm>

The Whiteley Clinic. (03/23/09). Anatomy of leg veins. <vein.co.uk/venous_anatomy_3_copy.htm>

The World Factbook. (03/05/2009). Russia. <https://www.cia.gov/library/publications/the-world-factbook/print/rs.html>

Too Me. (03/18/2009). ConiferousTrees Also known as "Evergreens" (Because they stay green all year). <www.nebo.edu/misc/learning_resources/ppt/k-5/coniferousrees.ppt>

Travel Muse (2009) Khodynka Arena Moscow, Russia. <travelmuse.com/pois/RU/48/attractions/khodynka-arena>

Tripadvisor. (2009). Moscow Grand Mosque. <http://www.tripadvisor.com/Attraction_Review-g298484-d573185-Reviews-Moscow_Grand_Mosque-Moscow_Central_Russia.html>

Victoria. (2005). Victoria Olives.
  <http://www.victoriapacking.com/olives.html>
Ways to Russia. (2002). Theaters in Moscow, Russia.
  <waytorussia.net/Moscow/Theaters.html>
Wikipedia. (05/07/2009). AIDS.
  <http://en.wikipedia.org/wiki/AIDS>
Wikipedia. (05/03/2009). Alternating current.
  <en.wikipedia.org/wiki/Alternating_current>
Wikipedia. (05/04/2009). Battery (electricity).
  <en.wikipedia.org/wiki/Battery_(electricity)>
Wikipedia. (04/15/2009). Canada men's national ice
  hockey team.
  <http://en.wikipedia.org/wiki/Canadian_national_
  men's_hockey_team>
Wikipedia. (05/05/2009). Cancer.
  <http://en.wikipedia.org/wiki/Cancer>
Wikipedia. (05/07/2009). Chinese New Year.
  <en.wikipedia.org/wiki/Chinese_New_Year>
Wikipedia. (05/09/2009). Coca-Cola.
  <en.wikipedia.org/wiki/Coca-cola>
Wikipedia. (04/12/2009). Colisee Pepsi.
  <en.wikipedia.org/wiki/Colis%C3%A9e_Pepsi>
Wikipedia. (05/05/2009). Corticosteroid.
  <http://en.wikipedia.org/wiki/Corticosteroid>
Wikipedia. (04/01/2009). Domodedovo Inter' Airport.
  <http://en.wikipedia.org/wiki/Domodedovo_Inter
  national_Airport>
Wikipedia. (12/03/08). Dormition Cathedral, Moscow.
  <http://en.wikipedia.org/wiki/Cathedral_of_the_D
  ormition>
Wikipedia. (04/20/2009). Electrolysis.
  <http://en.wikipedia.org/wiki/Electrolysis>

Wikipedia. (05/05/2009). Electromotive force.
    <en.wikipedia.org/wiki/Electromotive_force>
Wikipedia. (05/04/2009). Galileo Galilei.
    <http://en.wikipedia.org/wiki/Galileo_Galilei>
Wikipedia. (05/11/2009). Humans.
    <http://en.wikipedia.org/wiki/Human>
Wikipedia. (04/20/2009). Ice hockey.
    <http://en.wikipedia.org/wiki/Ice_hockey>
Wikipedia. (03/31/2009). Ice Hockey World
    Champions.
    <http://en.wikipedia.org/wiki/IIHF_World_Cham
    pionships#1993.E2.80.93present>
Wikipedia. (05/10/2010). Indra. <
    http://en.wikipedia.org/wiki/Indra>
Wikipedia. (02/22/2009). Ivan I of Moscow.
    <http://en.wikipedia.org/wiki/Ivan_I_of_Russia>
Wikipedia. (04/05/2009). Joseph Stalin.
    <http://en.wikipedia.org/wiki/Joseph_Stalin>
Wikipedia. (01/30/2009). Khodynka Arena.
    <http://en.wikipedia.org/wiki/Khodynka_Arena>
Wikipedia. (03/12/2009). Lomonosov Moscow State
    University.
    <en.wikipedia.org/Moscow_State_University>
Wikipedia. (04/03/2009). Lymphatic System.
    <http://en.wikipedia.org/wiki/Lymphatic_system>
Wikipedia. (05/07/2009). Magnet.
    <http://en.wikipedia.org/wiki/Magnet#Magnetic_
    metallic_elements>
Wikipedia. (05/12/2009). Martin Luther King, Jr.
    <en.wikipedia.org/Martin_Luther_King,_Jr.>
Wikipedia. (04/15/2009). Musical scale.
    <http://en.wikipedia.org/wiki/Musical_scale>

Wikipedia. (01/22/2009). Natasha Rostova.
<http://en.wikipedia.org/wiki/Natasha_Rostova>
Wikipedia. (03/07/2009). Rainbow.
<http://en.wikipedia.org/wiki/Rainbow>
Wikipedia. (03/14/2009). Russia Men's national ice
hockey team.
<http://en.wikipedia.org/wiki/Russia_national_ice
_hockey_team>
Wikipedia. (05/28/2009). Uranium.
<http://en.wikipedia.org/wiki/Uranium>
Wikipeida. (03/18/2009). Uzbekistan.
<http://en.wikipedia.org/wiki/Uzbekistan>
Wikipedia. (04/11/2009). Wonders of the World.
<http://en.wikipedia.org/wiki/Seven_Wonders_of
_the_World>
Wilderness-Survival-Skills. (2003-2009). How to make
a fire. <http://www.wilderness-survival-
skills.com/how-to-make-a-fire.html>
World Federation of Societies of Anaesthesiologists.
(2000). Update in Anaesthesia.
<http://www.nda.ox.ac.uk/wfsa/html/u12/u1213_
04.htm>
World Reviewer. (04/24/2009). Travel guide to the
Best Festivals.
<http://www.worldreviewer.com/travel-
guides/festival/>
World 66. (05/05/2005). Shopping.
<world66.com/europe/russia/moscow/shopping>
Yannzgob. (01/16/2009). Wikia Sports. CSKA
Moscow.
<icehockey.wikia.com/HC_CSKA_Moscow>

About the Author

I had become accustomed to writing since a young age either through the work I had studied throughout my life or when taking notes on daily activities. I enjoyed writing from as far back as it was as paper and pen. Because of my youth and reflectance to what's important within it I was to write my books. Being privileged to having an education I didn't want my knowledge to be lost and so I thought I should write down my interests. My interests were like everyone else's in what they know and what they are taught. I didn't want to lose my education I had received and thought to write down what I knew as stories. As my worked continued I realised I had a true gift for creativity.

I am very pleased to present my history and my interests within these books of mine. The main aim of the whole project was to bring positive aspects of life to everyday situations. These even included mental behaviour to change and better adapt or evolve our situations. We can all better something at sometime, may this be a temper problem, may this be an illness or suffering to another, this maybe how to congratulate another when there's nothing that can be offered. The path of many religions show to care for our neighbour, our brother, sister, family or friend member but at times we did not know how to approach difficult situations. Overall I hope to have shown that we should first smile and alongside make others smile.

There are a few factors to consider from my observations. I have included these statements to follow in both stories and I hope you can agree they are of importance to understand. They aid humanity to survive with strength and explore the unknown realities.

In both stories I mentioned to understand that 'Om' (Sanskrit scripture for the hymn of peace), this should be done from within and only used externally in meditation or drown out annoying sounds. The theme peace to be identified as the colour 'black', the theme of each other, every human being, and every animal as being that of blood, something representing love, and that is anything 'red', and most important to live in the 'light', light is life and we have peace and love to find and build for one another. Light is most important, some people including myself would like to represent this Light to also be known as God, whatever his name maybe. And lastly whenever you require power then to harness the thought of light and imagine that, also place hands together. Feel your heartbeat when tightening hands together. This doesn't need to be praying but just holding stability.

Well I thank every reader to have got to this point of my book. I hope you've really enjoyed it. I am to carry on working in life and fitness to inspire people to live improved lives and work with people that can benefit from my remedies. Live, love, laugh and as always explore peace.

Printed in Great Britain
by Amazon